Tess

Tess

An Outback Brides of Wirralong Romance

Victoria Purman

TULE
PUBLISHING

Chapter One

TESS HARRISON SCREWED up her pert, freckled nose. And then unscrewed it immediately. She hated being thought of as pert. Perky was worse. And cute? No freaking way.

As she shook her head adamantly, her blond ponytail swished at her shoulders.

"Uh-uh. Not gonna."

She sat on a porch swing sandwiched between her brother Harry and her new sister-in-law, Isabella. Harry's legs were the longest and he was keeping up a slow and steady rhythm, back and forth, back and forth. Tess's sneakered feet skimmed the stone underfoot.

Harry sipped his coffee, leaned forward to look at his wife. "Told you."

Isabella scoffed. "Tess, you've got to try again. You have a reputation to uphold."

"I do not."

"Do too," Isabella replied, her eyes widening as she cocked her head at her husband. "You can't let him win this one. Your pride is at stake. Your very position as an American." Isabella paused, her eyes narrowed. "You know, you've got to do it for the red, white and blue."

Harry laughed and rolled his eyes at his sister.

"Please feel free to step in anytime and stop me if I get the cultural references wrong," Isabella said. "I'm a true-blue Aussie, you know. Not like my husband or his weak-assed sister."

"Weak-assed?" Tess glared playfully at Isabella.

"Where's your spirit? Your people fought off the British and won independence, didn't they? Do it for the founding fathers and mothers and George Washington and ... Alexander Hamilton."

Harry gazed at his wife with a loving smile before nudging his sister's arm. "We saw the musical when we were back in the US for our honeymoon."

Tess sighed and took another look at the plate Isabella was holding out to her. It held a single slice of toasted bread. Not the whole wheat that Tess preferred, but something very, very white. It was the smudge of something that looked like a smear of asphalt that she didn't want to go near.

"She won't," Harry said. "If it's not peanut butter and jelly, Tess won't go near it."

Isabella cringed. "Now *that* sounds disgusting."

"You think a PB and J is disgusting, but you eat that?" Harry teased.

"It's Vegemite. It's a rite of passage that Tess will have to complete if she's going to stay here in Australia."

"Stay? I'm not staying, Iz. I'm here for a month to learn a little about Matthews Wines and then I'm going home to the land of PB and J."

Tess watched as Harry and Isabella continued their good-natured banter. Married for thirteen months already—well, twelve months in which they'd been apart after Iz had disappeared back to Australia, and then a month of wedded bliss—and they were a picture of happiness. Tess was so glad to be in Australia, in Wirralong more specifically, to see her brother's happiness unfurl. He was the first of the four Harrison siblings to get hitched and the whole family, including their father, had attended the wedding. She loved her brother and already adored her sister-in-law.

But there was no way on God's little green earth she was going to eat that black gunk. She quickly jumped off the porch swing and checked the time on her phone in an exaggerated fashion. "Oh, look. Is that the time? I'd better be off."

"Tess!" Isabella called after her. "It'll be waiting for you when you come over next time."

"Still won't eat it. I'm leaving now."

"Speaking of leaving." Isabella got to her feet and kissed her husband goodbye. "I've got people to marry. A local guy and his Spanish bride. So romantic."

Tess gave Isabella and Harry a backward wave as she strode to her car. She breathed in the eucalypts and the fresh Wirralong air. California had gum trees too, so their scent wasn't unfamiliar to her, but out here, in the wide open spaces of this new country that was still so unfamiliar to her, it was all fresh and exciting and an oh-my-God kind of thrilling.

She was in Australia. How had that happened so quickly?

She tooted three times and the house grew smaller in Tess's rearview mirror as she navigated down a dusty track to the main road that would take her back to Wirra Station.

When Harry had asked Tess to stay on a while in Australia after their family's business had bought into Matthews Wines, Tess hadn't imagined she was going to be living and working in such a magical place. It was going to be just the professional experience she needed to get her out of her rut of working for the family business, and help her to consolidate the ideas she had for her own future. A different country. The southern hemisphere climate. New colleagues to learn from and to share her experiences with. Back in Napa, she would always be little sister Tess, the youngest girl. The perky almost-youngest sibling—certainly the shortest even though she was five foot eight.

Here, somewhere new, she could be someone without all the baggage that came with being a Harrison. In Australia, she might have the chance to spread her wine wings.

She laughed at the idea. *Wine wings.*

Tess wound down her window so she could bring the sounds and the scents of this weird and wonderful country with her on the drive home. The wind whistled and flipped her long fringe all over the place. She hadn't had time for a haircut and really had to get around to calling Elsa's Hair Affair in the main street of Wirralong to get her hair done. She cranked up the volume on the car stereo and sang throatily and heartily for the ten-minute drive home.

As she turned off the main road and into Wirra Station, she tooted her horn at the figure in the front yard of the majestic main house. Maggie Walker-O'Connor, the owner and Isabella's oldest friend, stood smiling, holding a cup of coffee. Tess waved back and a minute later pulled up at her cottage. She sighed at the sight of it. A return verandah all around it meant every window was shaded against the scorching summer heat. Two wicker chairs were positioned by the front door, perfect for a glass of wine at the end of the day as the sun set in the west. A lavender hedge framed the three stone steps leading up to the verandah, deep red roses bloomed amongst them and the towering lemon-scented gums close to the house provided a perfect perfume for her arrival home. She'd moved in when Isabella and Harry had found their new home.

"Kudos to you, kid," she told herself as she grabbed her purse and got out of the car. "You managed to avoid Vegemite one more time." She laughed at how adamant Isabella was about it, as if it were a condition of her work visa or being her sister-in-law or something.

Her palate was refined. She tasted and sipped and measured and tested and spat out mouthful after mouthful of grape juice, of something that would soon be delicious. She couldn't sully her taste buds with that peculiar Australian concoction. What had Isabella been thinking?

But today she didn't have to do any tasting or think about wine. It was Saturday and Saturdays at Wirralong meant weddings.

Not that she loved weddings or anything. It was nothing like that. She'd grown up firmly of the belief that she didn't ever want any of it. When she'd announced her intentions one evening at the dinner table, her father had turned his disbelieving eyes to her.

"You're only fifteen years old, Tess. How can you possibly know what you'll want when you're an adult?"

Tess had been indignant. "I just know, Dad."

Across the table, Tess's mother had given her daughter a sly wink. Tess's chest had swelled with pride at this affirmation from her mother, at her insistence that she had known her own mind and would stand up for her choices.

All these years later, she still couldn't think of anything she wanted less than to commit herself to a person for life, to honour and obey—God, she hated that word—and give up on all her own dreams to make someone else happy.

Nup. No way. Not her.

But.

There was always a but.

Just because she didn't want to get married herself, it didn't mean she couldn't derive a great deal of vicarious

pleasure at watching other people leap into the great un-
known.

From her porch at Wirra Station, she now had a front-
row seat to the most romantic weddings in the state, as
brides and grooms—or brides and brides or grooms and
grooms—took the first step into the rest of their lives
together. Every Saturday afternoon, and often other times
too, it seemed as if she'd stumbled upon the final scene in a
variety of rom-com movies. She loved watching on as
families and guests negotiated the complex and emotional
dynamics of weddings. While each one, on the surface, was
the same—two people making a commitment to each
other—there were differences in each one that made them
fascinating to Tess.

Watching the wildlife. That's how Maggie's husband,
Max, had described it when he'd caught her out one day.

Tess hadn't understood what he'd meant at first. There
were lots of Australian expressions she was coming to grips
with and sometimes the accent still baffled her. "What's that,
Max?" she'd asked.

"You're watching the wildlife," he'd repeated with a grin.
"You might call it people watching. I've seen you sitting
there with your glass of wine. I've seen you cry, too, wipe
your eyes with a tissue you pull from your pocket."

She'd swallowed hard and waved his idea away. She was a
grown woman with a burgeoning wine career and zero
interest in getting married herself. What on earth would

make Max think she would become so emotional at the wedding of two people she'd never even met?

"Crying?" she laughed in response. "It's all these Australian native flowers and their strange pollens and blossoms that I'm not used to. They must be giving me allergies."

"Allergies," Max had repeated as if he hadn't believed her.

"I'll have to head to the pharmacist in Wirralong and buy some antihistamines. They should help. With the runny eyes, I mean."

Max was nowhere in sight that afternoon. He was probably with Bridie while Maggie was making sure all the last-minute details for the venue were in place. She took care of every detail, from catering to the marquee, to calming the mothers of the bride and all the floral arrangements that decorated tables and the wedding arbour.

Tess couldn't wait to see what that day's wedding was going to be like. She toed off her sneakers at the front door and went quickly inside. There was a bottle of riesling in the fridge and a wineglass with her name on it.

There was going to be a wedding today at Wirralong Station and Tess wasn't going to miss a minute.

Chapter Two

TESS HARRISON HAD always been a tomboy. She'd never worn princess costumes as a child or glammed up as a teenager. She'd never hankered after being a bridesmaid. And she'd never really been interested in doing anything other people might have viewed as girly once she'd hit adulthood. She had always been a jeans, T-shirt and sneakers kind of gal. And now, she worked in vineyards where there was never any call for heels or suits. She didn't bother with makeup (mascara and foundation simply sweated off when you worked outdoors) or anything too frilly or fancy. She wore practical clothes to work, comfortable clothes when she wasn't at work, and didn't fuss with hairdos or products, simply pulling her longish length blond hair up into a high ponytail every day (and she cheated and used dry shampoo when it looked a little in need of a wash).

So why was she such a fan of watching these great big girly extravaganzas?

When she crashed on the sofa at the end of a busy work week, desperately needing some comfort television, she binge-watched whichever reality wedding show she could find. Every new episode was filled with hyped-up crisis after hyped-up crisis. Family dramas and surly grooms, bridesmaids delirious from lack of food and brides nearly hysterical from the pressure of meeting everyone's expectations.

Of course, everything worked out in the end, which was what was so addictive about those programs. Love truly would conquer all, at least for as long as the program lasted, and that was good enough for her.

So when Tess moved in to the cottage at Wirra Station, she had to pinch herself at the thought of what she would be able to watch each weekend. Who needed to binge watch TV when you could watch real-life weddings happening right in front of your cottage? Wirra Station weddings had it all: cranky flower girls and page boys who were up way past their bedtime threw tantrums on the lawns, fainting bridesmaids (she'd seen it with her own eyes), proud fathers, sobbing grooms, happy brides and fussing mothers.

She loved watching the mothers of the bride hover and fix things as they waited nervously for their daughters to arrive. Each and every time, they caused a lump in her throat that seemed as if she'd swallowed a grape whole, and brought on her tears. Did the brides know how lucky they were to have their mothers by their side for their big day?

Tess would never have her own mother to fuss over her, to take her wedding dress shopping, to say no to the dress, and then finally, yes. She would have no assistance about the tastiest wedding cake or the floral selection or the perfect colour for the bridesmaids' dresses.

The idea of a wedding without her mother there was unthinkable to Tess. So once she'd graduated college, she turned all her focus to her career. But she hadn't become a nun. She'd had boyfriends in high school and then a couple of more serious relationships in college. But Steve had dumped her by text message and she'd rebounded into the arms of Brian.

They'd dated for two years, but Tess later realised she'd always known there was something not quite right about their relationship. He'd always been just too... well, too much. Too fixated on the idea of their future together that he ignored where they were actually were in their relationship. It was as if he was climbing a ladder and dragging her behind him. Her suspicions were crystallised when they'd flown to his hometown of Wilmington in North Carolina for their first Thanksgiving together. His mother had gleefully introduced her to the extended family as "Brian's fiancée" and then immediately after as "the mother of my five grandchildren" and she'd almost choked on the green bean casserole. Brian and his mother had hatched an entire plan for her life. By then, Tess's mother was ill and the idea of moving to North Carolina to live in the family home— another idea he'd sprung on her that weekend—was not something she would have done in a million years.

She'd sworn off guys for a long time after that, dating now and then but not taking anything too seriously. Twelve months before, she'd had a fling with a guy called Alex, whom she'd met in Oregon while working there, but she'd been careful to not let it get past being casual.

Was she looking for love?

What she was looking for was a miracle: love with no strings attached about who she was or what she wanted. She was waiting for a man who realised that being in love with her meant not pushing her to give up all she'd worked so hard for. It hadn't just been her experience with Brian that had made her cautious. Her own mother had warned her when she was young about the price women sometimes have to pay for trying to combine a family and a career. It had been the night fifteen-year-old Tess had announced at the dinner table that she wasn't interested in getting married.

Tess had been drifting off to sleep when her mother had quietly come into her room and closed the door gently behind her. Tess knew immediately that this was going to be a private moment between the two of them and was so happy about having this special time with her mom. With four kids, a demanding husband and a busy household to run, these one-on-one moments were treasured.

"Hey, honey," her mom had said as she laid a hand on Tess's leg.

"Hey." Tess had turned and looked up at her beloved mother. If she closed her eyes now, she could still see the room. Her single bed. The big open window that overlooked the vineyard in the distance. The walls, in a colour of light green she'd chosen herself, and her white sheets. Her sneakers had been heaped in a pile in the corner and the light from the digital clock radio on her bedside table cast a green glow in the dark.

"Honey, I want to talk to you about something."

"What is it, Mom?"

"About what you said at dinner ..."

Tess had watched her mother's expression become wistful.

"I wanted to say—and this is something your father won't understand, so let's keep it our secret—but I want you to know that I admire you for knowing what you want. Did you know I was a winemaker when I met your father?"

Tess had remembered her shock at the revelation. "I had no idea. You never said anything. You've never even worked on a vintage or ..."

Her mother had taken a deep breath and looked Tess clear in the eyes. "I love your father, I always have, but he came from a very traditional family and expected our marriage to be the same. I have never once regretted having children and I love you all, even when you're being grumpy teenagers. But after I married your father, I made the decision to stop working and leave the winemaking to him. We've made a very happy and successful life together, but I want you to know that I would make a very different decision now, if I had the chance for a do-over. You've got a fire in your belly about your life that maybe I didn't have. You see, getting married and settling down with a family changed everything."

"But why, Mom?"

"Because … times were different and I made my choices. But it doesn't have to be that way for you, Tess. I want you to dream big."

Getting married and settling down had changed everything.

Mary Harrison had died five years before of breast cancer and Tess had never forgotten that conversation and her mother's advice. As she got older, Tess had searched for signs that the world was changing, but continued to find evidence that backed up her mother's experience. California produced ninety per cent of all the wine consumed in the United States, but how was it that only one in ten vintners were women? Half of the graduates in Tess's oenology class had been female, but it was as if they'd gone back home and disappeared through the cracks. And for all the talk about women being able to have it all, Tess had never seen that actually work in real life.

So she'd vowed never to be one of those women who gave up on their big dreams. She was going to make it in a man's world—hell, she was going to change the world—to honour her mother.

Not even stumbling across the most accommodating and understanding man in the world—The Perfect Guy—would distract her from that ambition.

Lucky for her there was no such thing. In her experience,

The Perfect Guy had been as elusive as the perfect wine.

Her life was on track. She was an up-and-coming wine-maker. She'd flown halfway across the world to work at Matthews Wines, her family's latest acquisition. People listened when she talked about Baumé and oak and all things wine-related, and she had a bright future.

She was pulled out of her thoughts by the squawk of two black-and-white birds flying overhead and she watched them as they disappeared into the distance. The sky above was a clear blue and cloudless. Tess shifted her chair on the porch of her little cottage to move out of the stinging heat of the setting sun. Guests were arriving for today's wedding at The Woolshed and she didn't want to get sunburnt as she watched. She waved away a fly, took a sip of her wine and studied the guests. Isabella had filled her in on today's bride and groom, Slipper and Ximena.

"Besotted," Isabella had noted. "The adore each other."

Isabella was a marriage officiant—or celebrant as the Australians called her—so of course she saw the romance in everything.

Tess concentrated as the parents of the bride crossed the neatly clipped lawns and headed toward the copse of gums near The Woolshed. There was an arbour set up there, threaded with clipped runners of wisteria vines and dotted with white roses.

Tess looked over at the wedding party. Mother of the bride was anxious, she could tell. She rearranged her husband's tie, as if he were a schoolboy wearing one for the very first time and he'd got it wrong. She fiddled with the fresh flowers pinned to the arbour, which were already wilting in the heat. She adjusted the first row of the chairs set out in two sections—bride's family on the right and groom's on the left—creating just the slightest bit more leg room for those in the second row, while her husband watched patiently.

Yes, she was a mother about to see her daughter marry.

Tess stared into her wine for a long moment and swirled the liquid around in the glass. She was relieved that she would never have to look across a crowd of guests and try to ignore the mom-sized hole at her own wedding. There was nothing in the world that could ever fill it up.

Tess swatted away a fly and sipped her wine.

Across the lawn, the mother of the bride was urging the father of the bride to sit down on one of the plastic chairs reflecting bright under the dappled shade of the trees. More and more people were arriving, women wearing wrap dresses that swept open in the breeze; men in tailored trousers and cuffed formal shirts who were tie-less in the heat; young children running rings around their exasperated parents, finding the wide open space too tempting not to investigate.

And then a man in a dark navy suit. Prickles rose on the back of Tess's neck as he strode right past her cottage and crossed the lawns on his way to The Woolshed. *Oh, hello.*

His blond hair was short, like a military buzz cut, and his eyes were shielded by reflecting aviator shades. His slim-fitting jacket hung from wide shoulders and they must have found some extra fabric for those trousers because his legs were long. Tess got to her feet and stepped to the railing on the front porch of her cottage to get a closer look. She lifted a hand to her eyes to shield them from the afternoon sun and if she knew how to whistle, she would have—quietly to herself.

Then the man in the dark navy suit stopped midstride and looked across at her.

A nice face. A strong jaw, slightly shadowed with growth about as long as his hair. Tess lifted her chin and shot him a challenging look. Was it against the law in Australia to sit on your own front porch and watch people walk past? She didn't think so.

The man in the dark navy suit brought a hand to his aviator shades and lifted them. He took a good long look at her, as if wondering if he knew her from somewhere, and then he turned to continue walking over to the wedding, as if he'd been mistaken.

Chapter Three

CONNOR HAWKER KNEW who she was.

The woman sitting on the front porch with a glass of wine in her hand, feet propped up on the porch railing, trying to discreetly check out all the wedding guests. She was the winemaker Tess Harrison, who was out at Matthews Wines for a few weeks. News travelled fast in the wine industry. Back home in South Australia, he'd heard that a Californian conglomerate had invested in a small but interesting organic winery in Wirralong. When he'd seen a job advertised, he'd decided once again that a change was as good as a holiday.

And he'd needed a change.

He slowed his pace, watched her watching the other guests. He'd never met Tess, but he knew about her and her family's business. Her father, Charles, had for decades been a major player in the Californian wine industry, although word was he was stepping back a little to let his four grown children run the business. Tess was developing a reputation as a young gun with a palate that couldn't be beat and an instinctive knack for creating some of the most interesting wines in California. Some said the wine-making process was simply chemistry: a combination of good vines, the right soil, good growing conditions, climate, the right amount of water, and yeast to kick off the fermentation process. But he knew from experience that a lot of it came down to an individual winemaker. That knack, that palate, was what made a good wine great.

He'd researched Harrison's Wines before he'd accepted the job and right there, on the family's website, he'd seen her picture with the caption Junior Winemaker underneath it. That's why he'd recognised her just now, as fresh-faced in the flesh as she seemed to be in the photo he'd seen online. He thought for a minute as he slipped his sunglasses back over his eyes about the perfect word to describe her. Perky. Blonde. White teeth. Big brown eyes. Like an American cheerleader from every movie every teenage girlfriend had made him watch. She'd been smiling like she had the best job in the world and wasn't afraid to let it show.

Connor had worked all over Australia the past few years. The past three years to be exact. There was Margaret River in Western Australia and then the Hunter Valley in New South Wales—from one side of the country to the other. He was damn good at what he did—creating and managing the huge and complex irrigation systems at wineries—and he'd never be short of work in a country that had sixty-five winegrowing regions with more than twenty-four hundred wineries in an industry worth more than forty billion dollars. Work had never been the problem. Right now, his head was the problem.

So he'd landed in northern Victoria. Give or take a month, he'd worked four jobs in three years. Once he'd set up new irrigation systems, it was a good time for him to leave one place and find the next job. It suited him, this nomadic lifestyle. Just when he started to get comfortable somewhere, when he got to know the locals, when he found that somewhere that felt a little like home, he shook it off, packed up his truck and found the next job. He'd been feeling restless, itchy, when he'd seen the news about Matthews. He made a phone call and he had a job.

"If you're looking, we're hiring," Toby Matthews had told him. He'd met the garrulous winemaker back in South Australia during one vintage in 2010.

And that's how he'd ended up in Wirralong.

Connor was crossing the neatly clipped lawns of Wirra Station when some kind of sixth sense had forced him to look over at Tess. He had learned lately to trust that mysterious gnawing, that curiosity that set him on edge. He should have listened to it so many times before. Especially about his French fiancée, Juliette.

Ex-fiancée. Very ex-fiancée.

Looking back, there had always been something wrong with their relationship, although he'd been too fuckwitted to admit it to himself at the time. For instance, they could never agree on where they should live. She wanted to go back to France. He wanted to stay in Australia. And if they stayed in Australia, she wanted to live in Sydney, not the Barossa. He'd had to explain that there were no vineyards in that city. Hell, they had never even been able to decide about getting a damn dog.

He'd always wanted an old dog that would love him unconditionally, one that would come with him to work each day, that would trot after him happily down the rows of vines when he was testing moisture content. The kind of mutt that would fall asleep under the cool shade of the canopy the leaves created on the grass. He never got to have the wife or the home or the dog. Three strikes and you're out, he thought.

He trusted that tingling intuition now. If he'd listened to it three years before, he might not have turned out to be the idiot who'd thought Juliette would stay. Who was stood up at the altar.

He was now the kind of idiot who had tossed in his job working for one of the biggest wine conglomerates in the world to come work for one of the smallest wineries in Australia. He'd needed to get out of that kind of corporate winemaking and he'd been lucky enough to find a new job twelve hours and another state away from his mistakes. Juliette was back in France—or so he'd heard—and he was as far away from that disaster as he needed to be.

The last place he wanted to be was at a wedding. So what the hell was he doing at one?

It was all Eddie's fault. Connor had literally met him that morning. Connor had only arrived the day before and it hadn't taken long for him to unpack his car and move his few things into the small furnished apartment he'd rented in Wirralong's main street, two doors down from a hairdresser's called Hair Affair and a stone's throw from a pretty fancy-looking restaurant called Janu's.

Feeling restless, he'd got back in his car and checked out the town. He'd seen a sign pointing to Wirralong Oval and had not long after found himself at the cricket club bar with a cold beer and a new best friend.

In just half an hour, Eddie had convinced Connor to sign up for the Wirralong Bushrangers cricket team. Connor discovered Eddie was a winery worker, one of those salt of the earth types who wore a high-viz vest all day and kept local sporting clubs alive and kicking with every spare hour they had. Connor should have said no, should have resisted. He hadn't planned on getting involved in anything that remotely felt like a local community. Those ties only sucked you in, made it harder to leave. But Eddie was one of those blokes. And the Bushrangers needed an opening batter. Desperately.

"Mate, Spiller's going on his honeymoon to Thailand and Cam-bloody-bodia for four weeks. We need another opener or we're up shit creek. Come to the wedding tomorrow and meet him. It's a free drink at a stand-up reception," Eddie had told him. "I'll introduce you to the other players.

He'd love you to come along."

That's how Connor had found himself at Wirra Station on his first Saturday in Wirralong, wearing his best suit—his only suit—which might have still been a bit crumpled from the trip over hanging in its suit bag from the hook near the passenger door.

And that's how he came to be exchanging glances at twenty feet with Tess Harrison. It was her, all right. Blonder and even perkier than she appeared in photos. A heart-shaped face with high cheekbones. Her wide eyes were trained on him the way a hovering hawk might watch a mouse.

A woman sipping wine on a porch on a Saturday afternoon was on her day off. He could respect that. He wouldn't go over and introduce himself. He'd meet her on Monday, anyway, when he started work.

Connor averted his gaze but something made him look back. He lifted his aviator shades from his eyes, just enough to see the sun hit her honey-blond hair so it was shining golden in the setting sun.

So she was objectively attractive. He could admire a woman like that these days and not feel a thing. Just like some people swear off cigarettes or carbs or sugar, he had sworn off women. And it was going pretty well so far. One whole year and he hadn't gone near one.

He swore under his breath.

Twelve whole freaking months.

He turned away and strode with purposeful steps toward the little gazebo where a collection of white plastic chairs sat in neat rows, slowly filling with guests who'd arrived in dusty sedans and flat-top trucks. He took a seat in the back row, adjusted his glasses and didn't look back to the blonde with the legs, despite the almost overwhelming need to. After what seemed like hours, familiar wedding music played from a portable speaker somewhere and the groom turned. Every head in the crowd spun around to see the bride arrive and as they watched her walk down the grassed aisle, Connor whispered to himself, "Congratulations, Brad. At least your bride turned up."

Chapter Four

TESS HARRISON WAS leaning over the wooden bar in the tasting room at Matthews, her workboot-clad feet dangling, when Connor walked in bright and early on Monday morning. He lifted his aviator shades and slipped them on the top of his head as he stepped through the low doorway of the old stone building. As his eyes adjusted to the dim light, he spotted a pair of great legs. She wore khaki work shorts that rode up a little just above her knee and how could he not notice the tan line that stopped just below the curve of her quad? His mind raced to an image of whipped cream on a caramel pie. He looked away, turning his attention to the shelf above the narrow windows in the stone wall on the other side of the bar. For a moment, he studied the layers of dust on wine bottles older than he was.

"Good morning," he said finally.

Her steel-capped boots hit the old slate floor with a thud. She turned and blinked up at him. The polo top she was wearing featured a Matthews Wines logo on the left breast.

Up close, she was taller than he expected, almost up to his chin. That's what happens when you have such long—.

The legs. Stop thinking about her legs.

"Oh, hey there." It was kind of dim in the tasting room. Not much light seeped inside from the small wooden window set into the stone behind the counter and the ceiling was low, but that smile lit up the room. A smile that smacked him square in the solar plexus.

He cleared his throat. "I'm Connor Hawker."

Her lips parted and she made a little *O* shape with her cute mouth. Her eyes widened just the slightest bit and then she dropped her gaze to study the corkscrew in her right hand. She started tapping it against her palm, making a drum of her left hand. It made a rhythmic sound in time with his heartbeat.

"Connor Hawker. Right. You're our new—"

"Irrigation manager."

"We've been expecting you." Tess extended a hand and they shook vigorously, professionally. There was a strength in her grip. An assuredness. "I'm Tess Harrison."

"The winemaker," he replied.

"Junior winemaker," she corrected, and he wondered why she had.

They couldn't seem to let go of each other's hands, shaking in slow motion as they sized each other up.

"It's nice to meet you. I've heard a lot about Matthews. And Harrison's."

"You have?" She shifted her weight from one leg to the other. "I'm guessing you did your homework before starting this job, right? And I mean, why wouldn't you? Everyone around here is really thrilled you've come to work for Matthews. One look at your resume and everyone was blown away. Toby, especially. He said he worked with you somewhere. Was it Western Australia? South Australia? Anyway. You've worked in a lot of places, but there's a question I'd like to ask you. Why leave one of the biggest concerns in Australia to come work at this little place in Wirralong? Don't get me wrong, we're glad you're here and all, but people might think this is a step down for you. Or at least a sideways one."

Connor took a mental step backward as he adjusted the strap of his laptop bag, feeling exhausted just listening to her. The woman with the legs had barely drawn breath since he'd walked in to the tasting room and he wasn't sure which question to tackle first or if he should answer any of them at all.

"I'm interested in organics, Ms. Harrison," he said finally. That was part of the reason and that's all she was going to get.

She studied him. "You should call me Tess."

"Tess." He liked the sound of it on his lips.

Their fingers slipped away from each other. Connor smelled dust and yeast and cardboard boxes in the dim light of the tasting room. He stepped back and ran a hand over his hair out of habit, one that came back to him unbidden when he didn't know what to do with his hands. It was still a shock to him to feel it so short. He'd shaved it all off the day after what should have been his wedding day in an act of rebellion and he still enjoying the prickly feeling of the buzz cut. It had been like cutting off his past and he intended to keep it short to remind him every morning when he looked in the bathroom mirror that he was someone else now. Someone who'd left all that shit behind him. Someone who was starting afresh.

"We were sad to lose Bill, our old irrigation manager," Tess said as she slipped the corkscrew into her back pocket and walked through the low door out into the bright sunshine of the courtyard, beckoning him to follow. A big old peppercorn tree shaded the brick-paved space, which was surrounded by old stone buildings. "But his wife got sick and they've moved to Melbourne. They're closer to a bigger hospital and the medical specialists she needs, which is a relief, don't you think?"

"I was sorry to hear that," Connor said. "I hope she'll be okay."

"So does everyone here. I didn't know him all that well but he was as much a fixture of Matthews Wines as the American oak barrels."

"I've got big shoes to fill."

Tess glanced back over her shoulder. "Yeah, you do. But Toby wouldn't have brought you on board if he didn't have complete faith in you. I haven't known him that long but I already know he's an excellent judge of character, as well as wine."

They turned left at the corner of an old stone wall. Behind it, there was a low-roofed cottage with a glass door inset into the stone. The word 'Office' was inscribed in gold in the glass.

"Here we are," Tess announced and Connor followed her inside.

"Harry," Tess called as she took a left off the hallway. "Connor Hawker's here."

"Connor!" Another American accent. A tall bloke appeared and thrust out his hand. More firm handshakes. "Harry Harrison. Good to finally meet you."

Connor tried to see a resemblance to Tess. Maybe their height. And definitely their American-ness. Such white teeth. "It's good to be here."

"Hey, Toby," Harry called around him. "He's here. Connor, take a seat, won't you? Can I make you a coffee?"

"Yeah. Thanks. Black. Two sugars."

Harry worked the coffee pod machine on a cupboard in the corner of the room and put a steaming mug on the desk in front of Connor. He'd already had two cups this morning, but another one wouldn't go astray. He'd been up at the crack of dawn, as he always was, listening to the crows and the rosellas and kookaburras, the rustle of the trees in which the birds flitted and settled.

"Thanks," Connor told Harry. Tess at on the chair next to him and crossed one of her long legs over the other and in his peripheral vision he saw it jiggle.

Big footsteps and a booming voice. "Mate! Welcome to Matthews."

Connor got to his feet and reached out to shake another hand. Toby had wild grey hair and a huge cayenne pepper beard. He looked like a bushranger.

"Thanks, Toby."

Toby leaned against the wall by the doorway and Connor sat down behind his desk. They all looked at Toby. "It's good to have you here. It really is. Still can't believe we got you away from the big blokes in South Australia," Toby chuckled, "But I won't look a gift horse in the mouth."

Connor leaned back in his chair and lifted his chin in Toby's direction. "I learnt all I could heading up a whole crew and I thought it was time to get my hands dirty again."

"You've come to the right place. We don't have a big team. Harry and I are running the business side of everything, Harry more than me to be honest these days. He's the transition plan, aren't you, Harry? That's the good thing about selling a stake to someone else, Connor. I can think about doing more wine drinking and less of the hard work." Toby's big frame shook with laughter. "And Tess here is learning about the organic aspects of what we do, right Tess? And then she's going to steal all my secrets and take them home to the good old US of A."

"You bet I am," Tess winked at Toby.

Connor chanced a glance at Tess. She was feisty. He

sipped his coffee, hoping it might hide the smile he felt tugging at his mouth.

"If you need a desk, there's a spare one in the office next door, Connor. You can share with Tess."

Connor patted his laptop bag. "I'm pretty mobile these days. I can do most of what I need to do on my laptop. I can set up the irrigation schedules, track soil moisture and everything else right here."

"Jeez," Toby raised his eyebrows. "Old Bill had trouble using a mobile phone." He slapped his thigh and laughed boisterously. "Anyway, there's room with Tess if you need to get out of the heat. Our sales and marketing staff are up in the main street of Wirralong in a new office."

"Whereabouts?" Connor asked. "I've just rented a place in the main street."

"They're next to my wife Isabella's office. Wedding Belles," Harry said proudly. "She's Wirralong's resident marriage celebrant."

Maybe that's why Connor had had the mental blank. "Well. Can't wait to take a look around, get to work."

"We've brought you in at just the right time. As I mentioned during your interview, we need to modernise these irrigation systems and fast," Harry said. "It's damn dry out here and getting drier, which I'm sure is no surprise to you, but it sure was to me and Tess. I'd like you to come up with a plan for undergrounding it all."

Connor nodded. "You'll save water. And money. If you

deliver water directly to the root zone, you could potentially cut your water use by two-thirds."

"That much?"

Connor shifted in his chair, leaned his elbows on his knees. "You could potentially go from three megalitres per hectare per year to one megalitre."

"That's great for the environment," Tess said. Her leg jiggled. He tried not to notice. "But what about yields?"

"These new generation drop irrigation systems mean shorter watering times, less evaporation and better yields because the vines aren't competing with weeds and grasses."

Toby, Harry and Tess exchanged glances and nodded enthusiastically.

"We'd better get you to work," Toby bellowed. "But give us a minute, will you? Tess and I were about to taste a thirty-year-old bottle of shiraz. One of our first vintages."

Tess inched forward on her chair, tugged the corkscrew out of her pocket and handed it to Toby. There was a bottle on the table, covered in dust. Toby carefully peeled of the foil lid and spun the corkscrew around into the cork. It gave with a pop. He then held the bottle to his nose and sniffed, frowned and swore colourfully.

"It's off. It smells like a wet dog."

"It's corked?" Tess asked.

He passed the bottle to her and she breathed it in. "You're right. 1989 was such a good year, too."

Harry's phone sounded. Before jabbing the screen to

pick up the call, he said, "Tess, why don't you show Connor that desk? And Connor, you're invited to dinner Wednesday night at our place. Isabella insists. We all know what it's like to be new in town."

"Speak for yourself," Toby laughed.

"Follow me," Tess said with a quick smile. She stood and walked out.

And Connor did as he was told.

Chapter Five

WHEREVER HE LIVED, Connor needed to have a local coffee shop. Because he travelled light—stowing whatever he needed in the back of his four-wheel drive and hitting the road—he didn't ever have space for his own coffee machine. This had become a matter of some urgency because the coffee out of the pod machine out at the winery wasn't cutting it, no matter what flavour he'd tried. So, when he'd risen early on Tuesday morning, he'd gone in search.

He walked up and down the wide street twice. The grand main drag had clearly seen better days, but there were some hopeful signs. In its heyday, Wirralong had been a gold rush town for almost twenty years in the 1850s and '60s and many of the old buildings—although some were a little worse for wear—had grand façades and verandahs. Now, there were a few modern businesses mixed with some old, like the butcher and the greengrocer and a hardware store with displays of workboots and toolboxes out front, with high-viz clothing in the windows on mannequins with hairdos straight out of the 1970s. Moustache anyone? He made a mental note to swing by if he ever needed any work gear.

But on this warm January morning, there was only one place that looked like it dispensed caffeine. If he wanted his early-morning coffee fix, it was going to have to be the Outback Brides Coffee Shop.

For fuck's sake.

When he'd accepted the job at Matthews Wines, he'd had no damn clue that the whole town was obsessed with weddings and brides. It wasn't only the coffee shop. There was Wedding Belles, too, Harry's wife Isabella's office a couple of doors down in the other direction. When he'd tried to get another buzz cut the day he'd arrived, a simple five-minute clipper job in the only hair salon in town, the woman who ran the place had laughed and explained patiently to him that he just couldn't walk in on a Saturday without an appointment.

"On Saturdays we're chock-a-block with brides, mothers of the bride, matrons of honour, bridesmaids and flower girls. Sorry we can't fit you in. Come back when we're not so busy." She'd tapped on her computer's keyboard and studied the screen. "I can fit you in on Wednesday morning first thing. Does that suit?"

He'd politely thanked her and left. Wednesday morning was no good. He was already planning to be out in the vineyards undertaking soil tests early that day to avoid the burning heat from mid-morning on. So he arrived at the coffee shop just after seven o'clock when it opened for the day. The bell tinkled above him as he stepped inside.

"Good morning," called a woman standing behind the counter. She was about his mother's age and, like his mother, grey-haired and glowing with energy.

"Good morning." Connor smiled politely and removed his Akubra hat.

"What can I get you this fine morning, young man?"

He found her smile and her description of him kind of charming, despite himself. "I'll have a coffee thanks. Takeaway. Black with two sugars."

"Anything else with that?"

"No. Thank you. I'm good."

She raised a knowing eyebrow. "Far be it for me to blow my own horn, but everyone in town says my lamingtons are the best in the whole state of Victoria. Since you're new in town, you might like to give one the taste test."

She read his confused expression and she smiled generously as she lifted one of her creations and slipped it into a paper bag.

"Oh, don't worry. You know country towns. Toby Matthews was in here last Friday—white with two sugars and a buttered finger bun—and he told me he had a new irrigation manager starting this week."

Connor reached a hand across the counter. "Connor Hawker. Nice to meet you."

They shook warmly. "I'm Mrs Fairclough but everyone calls me Mrs F. Welcome to Wirralong."

"That's very kind."

While Mrs F busied herself making his coffee, Connor surveyed the array of cakes behind the glass on the counter. Jam tarts. Chocolate donuts. Rock cakes. Vanilla slices. Macaroons. Iced finger buns with shredded coconut sprinkled on the top. Connor decided that he could overlook the name of the country coffee shop if it meant an array like this every day.

A moment later, Mrs F put his coffee on the counter. "Be careful. It's a little hot, so I've doubled cupped it. It should stay warm all the way out to the winery."

"I appreciate that," Connor said. "See you tomorrow."

"I'll be here," Mrs F said with a smile. Connor took two steps toward the door and hesitated. She'd given him a complimentary lamington. He'd already had breakfast but maybe he should buy a few things and take them out to the winery for morning tea. It was the right thing to do to return the favour to Mrs F for her generosity and it was also the kind of thing the new guy should do for his colleagues, wasn't it?

"Changed my mind. I might grab a couple of things, Mrs F. Two iced finger buns, buttered, and a vanilla slice if you don't mind."

Mrs F grinned as if she'd known all along that he wouldn't be able to resist such temptation.

CONNOR ARRIVED AT the winery twenty minutes later to find Toby and Harry standing outside in the cool air nursing their coffee mugs.

"Morning." He handed them each a paper bag. The vanilla slice for Harry and one of the iced finger buns for Toby. He'd keep the other for himself and give the lamington to Tess. He wondered if she'd arrived yet.

"What's this?" Harry poked inside his bag.

"Breakfast with my compliments," Connor replied.

"Ah, I like a bloke who sucks up to the boss," Toby laughed heartily as he smoothed down his beard and looked inside the paper bag at Connor's offering. "This from Mrs F's?"

Connor nodded.

"A gift like this tells me you're in for a long career here at Matthews, my son. I bloody love a finger bun. Cheers, mate."

Connor had known Toby for years and he hadn't changed one bit, despite his success, and now his wealth from the Harrison buyout. Connor wouldn't have made the move to Wirralong if he hadn't been sure he could work with Toby.

And Harry? He seemed like a good guy too, even if he came from the kind of money Connor could only imagine. He seemed down to earth, smart but not in your face, a good businessman but not one who put people last when he was doing the sums about what made a successful business in the first place.

"I'm going to live to regret this," Harry said as he bit into his vanilla slice. "Oh, hell." His eyes widened. "This is incredible."

Connor looked around. "Tess here?"

"She's just pulled up," Harry mumbled with a mouthful of custard.

Tess's vehicle was a white ute, decorated with Matthews Wines logo on the doors. She turned the engine off, hopped out, slammed the door and regarded the three men with knitted eyebrows. Connor kept eyes front on her face. *Do not look at her legs. Repeat: do not look at her legs.*

"What's going on here?" she asked, a small leather backpack hanging on one shoulder, her hands propped on her hips. How was it that she seemed to bring the sunshine with her wherever she went? It radiated from her tanned face, her brown eyes, and her hair caught the light and shone.

"Breakfast," Toby announced. "Courtesy of Connor."

Harry was still savouring his vanilla slice and did nothing by grin.

Connor handed her a paper bag. "This one's for you."

She took it and thanked him. "What is it?" She lifted out the cake and examined it.

"It's a lamington."

"That doesn't help me." She sniffed it. "Chocolate? Coconut?"

"It's a square of sponge dipped in chocolate and then

covered in shredded coconut. It's the best in the whole state of Victoria, apparently."

She slipped it back in the bag. "You been talking to Isabella? Harry?" She turned to her brother. "Is he in on this, too?"

Harry only smiled.

Connor scratched his head. "In on what?"

Tess blew out a frustrated breath. "Isabella is on a mission to get me to fall in love with Australia. Tim Tams I can do. Not so fond of her roast lamb but, you know, it might grow on me. But Vegemite? Nope. Never in a million years. And now you turn up with this ... this Australian cake thing." She eyed him suspiciously.

"It's just a cake, Tess," Harry mumbled. "Chill."

"Hmm," she replied.

Connor didn't know what he'd got in the middle of and decided that not buying into it was his best course of action.

"Your coffee smells good," she said, eying Connor's takeaway.

"It is good. It's from that ..." He cleared his throat. "Outback Brides Coffee Shop."

Tess kicked the dirt with a steel-capped boot. "And if I didn't live in the middle of nowhere I'd have a local coffee shop, too." She stomped past and pushed the door to the office open with two flat palms. It banged behind her.

Toby looked at Harry. "What's up with Tess?"

"Not a clue, pal." He brushed pastry crumbs from his

shirt. "She might be my sister but she's a woman first and sometimes I find it best not to ask."

WHEN CONNOR WALKED into their office a few minutes later, Tess looked across at him as if she'd been caught with her hand in the till. She was devouring the lamington he'd given her. The evidence was plain: smudges of chocolate were smeared all over her full lips and sprinkles of coconut decorated her desk like tiny snowflakes. Her eyes flared wide and a hand flew up to cover her mouth.

"I was …" she mumbled.

Connor held up a hand as if to say, no need to explain. He put his coffee on his desk, plugged in his laptop and sat down, pretending that he was checking his emails. But he was thinking something else entirely. *Holy shit.* Tess's mouth covered in chocolate. It sent him to places in his mind that he had no right to go. Especially not with her. Naked places. Down and dirty places.

He gulped down the rest of his coffee and stared at his screen.

Was it a moment later or an hour? It felt like three days when Tess came to the side of his desk and perched her butt there.

"Connor."

"Yep?" He kept his eyes fixed on his screen.

"Sorry about that. I started the day in a shitty mood and I brought it with me all the way from Wirra Station. I rage sang to very loud songs on the drive here, which usually works. It's something I learned in college. At first it was Nirvana, then System of a Down. And usually Foo Fighters hit the spot but nope, none of that helped me today at all. You know when you just get up on the wrong side of the bed sometimes? That's what happened to me this morning. It was hot last night and I was tossing and turning like a pig on a spit. So, no hard feelings, okay? It was nothing to do with you. In fact," she tapped her fingers on his desk like a drumroll. "That ... what did you call it?"

"Lamington."

"Right. That lamington really hit the spot. Turns out it was just what I needed. Chocolate. So thanks."

"You're welcome." Connor didn't look up until Tess had turned her back and returned to her desk.

Chapter Six

"SOMETHING SMELLS GOOD." Tess opened the door off the porch and walked directly into the kitchen at Harry and Isabella's new home. The property was a short ten-minute drive from Wirra Station, set on acreage amongst vineyards and open fields. Harry and Isabella had bought it before they'd gone back to the states for their honeymoon and had now begun their married life together in it. It might have felt brand new to them but it already seemed lived in, and loved, to Tess.

"Hey, Tess," Isabella looked up with a warm smile. "It's roast lamb. I've had it slow cooking all day in the oven." She sighed dreamily as she took in her new kitchen with its gleaming silver oven. "You know, I've worked weekends a long, long time and I'm used to it. I really am. It's what you have to accept about being a marriage celebrant."

Tess walked over to the kitchen bench and presented her sister-in-law with two bottles of wine, before squeezing her with a tight hug. "'Marriage celebrant'. I still can't get used to hearing that. You'll always be a marriage officiant to me."

Isabella shrugged. "Different country. Same thing.

Thanks for the wine. The thing I love about having days off during the week is that I can do this for the people I love who've been working hard all day." She waved a hand over an array of salads and freshly baked bread set out on the bench in a tantalising display.

"And we'd love you even if it was macaroni cheese," Tess assured her. "But I'm glad you're embracing your inner domestic goddess. Anytime you want to go all happy home-maker, let me know. I'm always so exhausted when I walk in the door that cooking is the last thing on my mind. Any-thing to save me cooking a meal and I'm in."

Isabella opened the oven door to check the lamb. For a moment she disappeared in a cloud of steam. "And I know you're too polite to comment on my choice of meat, but you know I'm on a mission to turn you and Harry into true-blue Aussies. If it can't be Vegemite, it might have to be this. It's Australia's favourite dish, don't you know."

"You might have more chance turning Harry into an Aussie than me," Tess quipped. "He has a vested interest in becoming Australian. If you get what I mean and I think you do. Me? I'm only visiting, remember?"

"Remind me again how long you are planning to stay?"

"For a month, at least for this trip. Then I'm flying home to take all I've learned and put it into practice back in Napa. I've got an idea I want to float by Harry and my father and the entire board at the February meeting and I need to be back home to do it. I'll have one shot and I don't what to blow it."

"What plan?" Isabella slapped her oven mitt on the bench and popped her hands on her hips. "Is it about Harrison's? Selling Matthews Wines into the States? Harry hasn't mentioned a word about any plan. Tell me everything."

"It's hush hush for now. Which means it's still not quite fully formed in my head yet, but you'll be the first to know. I promise. Or maybe Harry will be, but he'll no doubt tell you everything so you'll be the second to know, but you're family so … It'll be good, I promise."

Isabella threw Tess a playfully mournful look. "Are you sure you have to go back home to make this presentation to the board? Can't you do a video call? You've only just arrived and I don't want to let you go just yet. We really love having you here, Tess."

Tess hadn't known Isabella that long, but what she did know about her was that she hadn't had a happy childhood. Isabella had been left on her own at the age of eighteen by a mother who hadn't wanted her in the first place and she'd been forced to make her own way ever since. And now, she had a family. A modern family. Maggie and Max and the Smart Ladies Supper Club women and the whole of Wirralong. And Harry, obviously. There were also two sisters-in-law, a brother-in-law and a father-in-law who all thought Isabella was the bee's knees, even if she had lured Harry away from the US. Tess believed Isabella was fortunate in one respect, in that she had never known how smothering it could be to come from a family so big, and how hard that made it to break out on your own. Especially when your family were the Harrisons of Napa Valley.

"I really have to be there in person. Because I need to see the whites of their eyes—and they need to see the determination in mine—when I make my pitch." Tess paused. "It's home to me, Iz. And as tempting and as beautiful as Wirralong is, with you and Harry and this perfect house, I know my dream will come true somewhere else. I've always known that."

Isabella looked sideways at Tess as if she didn't believe her.

Tess laughed at her expression. "It's true! You wait until you hear it. Then you'll know what I mean."

Tess looked around at the house. It really was perfect. She made a series of mental notes; she might start recreating it at a house of her own one day. The stone-and-brick cottage was set amongst established gardens filled with roses and lavender and hawthorn bushes and what Isabella had assured Tess were hardy Australian native plants that wouldn't whither under the blazing Australian summer sun or scorching north winds. On the east side of the house, towering gum trees were home to two koalas that nestled dozily amongst the branches during the day and fought screechingly at night. Or maybe they were doing something else, she wasn't sure. Inside, polished floorboards and restored furniture mixed with a brand-new white kitchen and a pine dining table with twelve chairs. Each of the four bedrooms was fitted out with a queen-sized bed, the most comfortable mattresses Tess had ever slept on, and coverlets and pillows that actually matched. When Harry and Tess had bought the house, they'd insisted she move in with them. But she'd graciously declined. As much as she adored the place and its location—and especially Harry and Iz—she didn't want to live with a newly married couple, no matter how much she loved them both.

"Look, I've been to California," Isabella smiled. "It's lovely. And your family winery and the whole property is incredible. But …"

"What about California?" Harry strode into the kitchen and made a beeline for his wife. He pulled her into his arms, gazed into her eyes and stared at her.

It was a new thing for Tess to see her brother so lovestruck and so unashamed about showing it. And the way he was looking at his wife right then was the stuff perfect guys were made of. Harry? Who knew?

"Hi, Harry," Tess interrupted when it seemed he was going in for a passionate kiss. She didn't need to see that.

He looked up, startled. "Brat. Long time, no see."

"Bro," she replied.

"Got those tasting reports done yet?" he asked, his eyes narrowing.

"Leave me alone. I'm on my own time right now. And

last time I looked, you weren't the boss of me."

"You two," Isabella laughed. "Leave it at the office. You Harrisons are so competitive."

"Are not," Tess replied.

"Are not," Harry added with a smile.

"Are too," Isabella said, louder than both her husband and her sister-in-law. She grabbed a tea towel from the stove handle and flicked it at Harry's ass.

"Hey," Harry laughed as he sidestepped out of the way. "You're going to pay for that."

Isabella cocked an eyebrow. "I damn well hope so."

"Settle down, you two." Tess rolled her eyes. "This is hardly the impression you'll be wanting to make on our new irrigation manager. What time's he supposed to be here, anyway?"

"Any minute. What do you think of him?" Harry screwed the cap off one of the bottles Tess had brought and poured her a glass.

"Connor?" Tess hoped her voice hadn't come out as a squeak but was suspicious that it had. "He seems … fine."

Fine. Yeah, fine was the word. Damn fine. Objectively, sexy as hell.

When Connor had walked into the tasting room that Monday morning, Tess had almost swallowed her tongue when she realised he was Navy Suit Guy from Saturday's wedding. If he'd looked damn good in a suit that day, and work gear out at the winery yesterday when he was smeared with the deep earthy brown Wirralong soil, he looked positively scorching in plain jeans and a shirt. She wasn't sure what exact colour his hair was, given it was buzz cut—dark blond or maybe brown?—but his eyes were sapphire blue and the dark stubble on his chin was almost as long as his hair. Up close in the cellar door, surrounded by old wine and cartons and the yeast smell embedded into the stone walls, she'd been momentarily lost for words when he'd walked in and introduced himself.

And then yesterday, when he'd come into her office first thing, she'd honestly tried not to, but had noticed things about him. She was a people watcher, an observer. He'd had three more cups of coffee and skipped lunch. He worked for half-hour stretches in various positions while he was catching up on some of the technical reports Bill had left for the handover: he typed really fast and loud on the small keyboard on his laptop; he paced around the small space between his desk and the wall while flipping pages, before sitting back in his chair with his boots up on the desk while reading.

She'd been relieved when Toby had taken him out into the vineyard in the early afternoon for a look around. She needed time to breathe and get her head straight. He was the reason she hadn't finished the tasting notes she'd been promising Harry for the latest vintage back home. She'd brought some vague thoughts with her when she'd come to Australia and now the marketing department—her brother

Everett—was breathing down her neck. How the hell was she supposed to concentrate when she had been sharing a very small space with Connor Hawker?

Not that she was vaguely or remotely interested in anything about Connor other than his work ethic and his soil test reports. Sure, he had nice arms and was super tall, but his hair was way too short and he'd barely said more than a few words to her since he'd arrived on Monday. In her experience, the strong silent types were way overrated. And yes, bringing her a cake was a nice gesture. She'd found it utterly and completely delicious and it had been exactly the chocolate fix she'd needed for her premenstrual stress. Her period had arrived by lunchtime yesterday, which was when she'd realised why she'd carried her shitty mood all morning. It happened every month and every month she forgot about the angries she got in the days before. Damn period, she thought. It seemed like such a waste of energy every month, not to mention painful and, frankly, socially annoying.

"Tess?" Isabella asked. "So, he's … fine?"

Tess shrugged. "Yeah, sure. He's fine. He's friendly in that laidback Aussie way. If you like that sort of thing. I read somewhere that Aussies in the bush don't open their mouths very wide when they talk in case flies crawl in. Is that true?"

Isabella nodded. "You've seen some of our flies. What do you think?"

Tess shuddered. She had purposefully steered the conversation away from Connor. There were things she was feeling slightly confused about. It wasn't just the lamington the day before. He'd brought her a takeaway coffee this morning. She'd squelched down the urge to hug him when he'd presented it to her, which was of course not appropriate in the office, but the takeaway was so much better than the coffee pod kind Harry insisted on making in his office.

Tess fanned herself. Why was she hot all of a sudden? It must be her thoughts about coffee.

"Harry says he's got a good feeling about Connor. Do you?"

"Sure. A good feeling," Tess conceded, which seemed to make Isabella inordinately happy.

"I'm glad we could do this for him tonight." Harry poured Isabella a wine and passed it to her. She thanked him with a lingering kiss. "He doesn't know anyone in town except us and a few blokes he met at cricket practice. As if that's a real game."

"Cricket," Tess scoffed and shook her head.

From across the kitchen bench, Isabella gasped. "You just wait. Before you know it, I'll have you both sitting in the shade at Wirralong Oval cheering on the Bushrangers. There's nothing like a game of cricket in the Australian summer. In fact, I've just had a brilliant idea. Let's make a date for next Saturday. I have a morning wedding and then another at two, so I should make it there before stumps. We could get a session in together."

"What is your wife talking about?" Tess winked at Harry.

"Watching cricket is like meditation. You'll see," Isabella called out. "It calms the soul."

"More like bores you senseless," Harry muttered under his breath.

Tess drummed her fingers on the kitchen bench and sipped her wine. It was a fruity riesling. One of her favourites. She hoped the mouthful would help tamp down the niggling restlessness that was making the pit of her stomach gurgle. Where was Connor? Couldn't they get this thing over with already?

Then she chided herself. She had to concede that he was new in town and they'd all be working closely together. Welcoming someone into your home was common in close-knit winemaking communities. The work was intense at times, and it was best to get to know each other before any tension boiled over. She should have more sympathy, she knew that. She understood what it was like to be alone in a new place, not knowing anyone, not understanding the dynamics of the friendships and networks and allegiances of a new town or a new city. She'd experienced that when she'd left Napa to study winemaking, and then again when she'd worked her first summer job at a winery in Oregon.

When she'd arrived in Wirralong, on a whim as much as anything (she'd really, really wanted to pet a koala), she'd had to, in effect, start all over again. And that's where Isabella had stepped in. Her new sister-in-law had welcomed Tess into her own circle of friends—Maggie and Elsa and

Serenity and Dr. Holly, Holly's friends Jasmine and Jacinta, and the new English woman Lady Emmaline Grayson. Tess had never met anyone vaguely royal before or, she should clarify, somehow vaguely—by dint of her title—twelve steps removed from the Royal Family. No one could figure out why Lady Emmaline—or Emmaline as she insisted everyone call her—was still in Wirralong when the world was her oyster.

Tess had quickly become part of their hilariously named Smart Ladies Supper Club. They'd managed to entirely miss the word *wine* from the name, and the regular meetings had become as much about wine appreciation as anything else. No one else worked in the wine industry, which made it fun for Tess. Her new friends didn't want expansive tasting notes explaining citrus notes or tannins: they just wanted each other's company and camaraderie.

And now Wirralong was opening its arms to another newcomer.

There was a knock at the front door. Isabella was making a salad and Harry was reaching for fresh wineglasses from one of the overhead cupboards, so Tess hopped off the high stool at the island bench and walked to the back door.

She opened the door, stepped back. "Hey," she said, attempting to sound breezy to fight the flip-flopping down low in her belly. "I see you found it okay?"

"Yep. No problems." Connor's boots clicked on the stone floor as he came inside. He held up a huge bunch of flowers with white and purple tissue wrapped around the stems. And as Tess stared at how beautiful they were, he said quickly, "These are for your sister-in-law."

Nice manners, she thought with an appreciative nod in his direction. He'd changed out of his collared shirt into a polo, and polished brown leather boots poked out from the legs of his clean, albeit faded, denims. She'd changed out of her work clothes too, into a sleeveless floral dress that skimmed her knees and bared her arms. His gaze dropped to her legs and lifted quickly.

"Come on in then. Isabella is putting the final touches to dinner and Harry is deciding what wine we're going to open next, aren't you, Harry?"

"Cheers," Connor said. The tissue paper rustled in his hand. His footsteps sounded on the floor. She hoped she was the only one who could hear her heart thudding.

"Hey, Connor," Harry called out from the kitchen. "Welcome."

Tess watched Connor as he looked around the space, taking it all in. It was perfect to her: the country-style kitchen, the long dining table and the living area at the other end with its soft leather sofas, throw blankets in the same shade as the paint on the walls, and patterned rugs. He probably only saw the big screen TV that sat atop a Balinese cabinet in the far corner.

Harry walked forward and the two men shook hands. "This is my wife, Isabella Martenson."

"Nice to meet you, Connor. Welcome to Wirralong."

He gave her the bunch of flowers. "Thanks for the invite. I appreciate it."

"Oh, that's so nice of you." Isabella sniffed the blooms. "They're gorgeous. Thank you."

Tess hung back, just out of his line of sight, watching him, this stranger in a strange setting. He ran a palm over his buzz cut and cleared his throat. She bit back the urge to talk—for once—and people-watched instead. Harry, Isabella and Connor seemed perfectly fine with the lull in the conversation. Maybe it was an Australian thing. Specifically, an Australian country thing that even Harry had acclimatised to. Maybe she had to be less American and more … laid back.

"I hear you've joined the Wirralong Bushrangers." Isabella arranged the flowers in a vase she had fetched from a cupboard by the sink.

"I don't know how, but they've roped me in. I'm playing my first game this Saturday. To be honest they're a bit desperate for players. I reckon I'm the youngest bloke in the senior team." Connor sauntered over to the island bench and leaned against the counter top. He was kind of super tall and that voice of his had a beautiful depth and tone to it that reminded her of muscat.

"Ah, the Bushrangers have been desperate for another bat for years. It's hard. A lot of people come through but they don't stay long, only around vintage." Isabella and Connor drifted into an easy conversation about the finer points of things Tess had no clue about. She wasn't really into sports.

Not basketball or NFL or hockey or any of the things some of her friends were obsessed with. Her obsession grew on vines. Her obsession developed and formed in barrels and was poured from bottles.

"Tess?"

She'd been lost in her own thoughts—and okay, sure, watching Connor—when she realised someone had said her name.

It was Harry. "Tess? A refill? They were all staring at her. Harry with a confused frown. Connor with an expression that gave nothing away. And Isabella. Her sister-in-law's eyebrows had risen into arches and she was subtly cocking her heard toward Connor. In a few seconds they had a long, silent conversation:

He's hot.

Sure. He's objectively hot. So what?

So you might have some fun.

Definitely don't need to have a man to have fun.

That's true.

And you know I'm going home in a few weeks and I'm definitely not interested in any man right now.

You sure about that? You're blushing.

Am not.

Are too.

Stop thinking at me.

Tess cleared her throat. "Sure. Let me pour the wine."

AFTER DINNER AND coffee, Isabella urged Tess and Connor out onto the deck while she and Harry cleaned up.

"Go. Show Connor the view. We'll tidy up in here and be out in a minute."

"Come on, Connor," Tess urged him. "It really is spectacular out there."

"Sure." He opened the door leading out to the deck and waited for Tess to go first.

She walked over to the wooden rail and looked out at the vista made golden in the late evening light.

There were paddocks filled with rolled hay bales and in the distance, on a neighbouring property, the incongruous outlines of alpacas. On one side of the house there was a perpendicular row of pine trees, their rich brown cones lying in the grass underneath like confetti. Tess sipped her wine and breathed deep. When she got back home, she should definitely find a house with a view something like this—except it would be filled with vines of course—and she would sit on a deck almost exactly like this every morning with her first coffee of the day and her bowl of homemade muesli, and survey her kingdom.

"What do you think, Connor?"

A long pause. "Spectacular."

Tess turned and held her breath at the look she saw on his face.

Chapter Seven

H IS EYES FLASHED hot and there was a flickering in his tense jaw. He lifted a hand and rubbed it over his spiky hair and suddenly Tess's mouth was dry. That gurgling in her stomach was back, but it couldn't be hunger. She'd eaten heartily and had even gone back for extra potato salad. She felt kind of sick and gripped the rail to steady herself.

This should not be happening. She hadn't had that much to drink. Two glasses. She'd been careful, always had. An up-and-coming winemaker, with a plan going forward for a long future in the industry, couldn't go around getting pulled over by the police for drink driving or, God forbid, doing someone damage on the roads.

What was going on with her? She turned back to the view. It was a safer bet than looking into Connor's eyes, that was for sure. He took up a spot next to her and out of the corner of her eye she noticed him looking at the view as well. If she leaned slightly to the left, she would bump into him. Her back stiffened. Up close like this, she could smell his aftershave. Something piny and fresh. Or maybe that was the pine trees. She couldn't tell.

He seemed happy to stand in silent contemplation.

"So, Connor Hawker, how are you settling in to Wirralong?"

"Pretty well." He flicked her a quick smile and then looked back out to the view. "So far."

"That's great. You mentioned you're living on the main street?"

"Yep."

"It's a pretty cute old town. I love the wide streets and all the historic buildings. It's so different from California. Have you travelled much? Have you ever been to the States? Or Europe maybe?"

"I've been to the south of France. And Italy. South Australia is starting to grow a lot of Italian varieties and styles, so a few years back I went over with a delegation of winemakers to take a look at them in their home soil."

"That's so interesting," Tess said. "Some of the Napa Valley growers have had luck with barbera and grignolino."

Connor turned to her. "The South Australians are having a go with montepulciano, nero d'avolo and fiano varieties, and a few others."

"I love a fiano. They're so aromatic."

"It's early days and none of those varieties can compete with rieslings and chardonnays when it comes to consumer taste, but we have a Mediterranean climate back home, and it's only getting drier, so winemakers and people like me are thinking out of the square."

Something happened to his eyes when he was talking about wine. They shone brighter. His mouth turned up a little at the corners. His shoulders seemed broader. He was comfortable on his home conversational turf. She got it.

"California's had drought, too. That's something my state and your country share, right? So, let me fill you in on what I know about Wirralong. There's only one pub and it's okay if you like fries and an overcooked steak. Obviously you've found the best coffee place already. Oh, and there's Janu's. Have you eaten there yet? Of course you haven't. You've only just arrived. I hear it's amazing and Harry says the wine list is to die for. Winemakers from fifty miles around come to Wirralong just to eat there. It's definitely on my bucket list while I'm here, that's for sure. Since I've already petted a koala, I can cross that off my list. Hey, maybe you can tell me: they sleep all day and make a huge, screeching racket at night. Why do they only fight at night? Is it some nocturnal marsupial thing?"

Connor's face split in a grin and he turned away in what was clearly an attempt to hide it.

"What's so funny? I know I'm right on the science. I looked it up. They *are* marsupials. They have a pouch to carry their young. And yeah, I know already that they're not actually bears."

He looked back at her. Her heart thudded. He was so damn handsome when he smiled.

"That nighttime screeching they're doing?"

"Yes! That's what I want to know about. What's up with that?"

"They're not fighting, Tess." Connor leaned in, looked right into her eyes and suddenly the palms of her hands were damp. His eyes were blue. Really blue. Something flipped in her belly.

"They're fucking."

"Fucking. Wow." Tess exhaled the huge breath that had become trapped inside her. The way he'd said the word, slow and teasing, reminded her that the koalas were probably having more sex in one night than she'd had in a whole year. "That's some great sex those guys are having up there on those really flimsy branches. I suppose it adds to the thrill, right? 'Gah, you'd better come quick. I could fall and plunge to my death any second here.'"

He laughed and it was deep and intensely pleasurable. Goose bumps prickled the back of her neck and she lifted a hand to rub them away. The sound seemed to seep right inside her, warming her like an old brandy from her father's cellar.

Connor turned and leaned back on the railing. His lips quirked in a smile, longer this time. "You're a long way from home, Tess Harrison."

"I'm a big ocean away, that's for sure."

"Do you miss it?"

"Not on evenings like this. I mean, look at the scenery." But she wasn't looking at the view.

"It's not bad at all," Connor replied. And he wasn't looking at the view either.

"It's all Harry's fault. He followed his heart right here to Wirralong, to Isabella. It's a long story, but they actually met in Las Vegas a year before and—can you believe it—they were married by an Elvis impersonator. But she ran off the day after the wedding and it took him a whole year to track her down. She was right here all along and … that's where he is now, too. We don't know if he's ever coming home."

Tess was still chuckling as she finished recounting Harry and Isabella's love story, when she realised Connor wasn't laughing. Not even at the Elvis bit?

His back had stiffened. "She did what?"

"It wasn't because she didn't love him or anything like that. Anyone who sees them together can see how totally devoted they are. They just had some … stuff … to sort through. Harry doesn't hold a grudge anymore, obviously, so how can I? But it wasn't the perfect start to married life, I have to admit. She worked hard to win me over. And to let you in on a secret, I think she's still working hard. But if she wants to bribe me with dinner, I'm in for as long as I can play it."

Connor shifted abruptly, turning away from her. Tess watched him. Maybe he was counting the hay bales that sat like enormous golden rolled-up blankets in the paddocks surrounding the house.

"So anyway, when we bought into Matthews, I came

down here to meet the girl who'd stolen Harry from us and then I saw Wirralong and I decided to stay a little while, to meet with Toby, to get a feel for the operation down under."

"How long's a while? When are you heading back home?"

"A few weeks."

He looked at her curiously. "You won't be here for vintage? Judging by what I've seen out in the vineyards this week, we're about three weeks away. You've come all this way and you're going to miss that?"

"I've got things I need to deal with back home. Some stuff I can't delay." Tess needed to turn the conversation away from herself. She nudged him with an elbow and he flicked a gaze down to where her elbow had touched his chest.

"So, what about you? What's your story? Where were you born? How did you get involved in this crazy business we all love so much?"

Connor shifted his weight from one hip to the other. Then he looked out to the hay bales. Birds twittered in the gum trees and the setting sun was creating long shadows and pink streaks in the eastern sky. She was beginning to learn that nothing he did was fast or spontaneous. "It was time for a change of scene from the Barossa," he said finally.

"You worked in the Barossa? Wow. That is definitely one of the places on my bucket list. I've done the Rhone Valley and even Champagne. I've been to the Finger Lakes in

Connecticut and tasted ice wine. I've worked vintages in South Africa and Oregon but I've never been to the Barossa. How far is it from here? Maybe I can drive over for a weekend and do some tasting."

Connor laughed.

"Probably not, unless you want to spend twenty hours in the car there and back."

"Really? I hadn't thought it would take quite that long."

"You do know how big this country is, right?"

"Well, sure. About as big as the States, give or take a state or two."

"Tess," he said and paused and damn it, she liked the way he said her name, long, like a drawl. "The Barossa is about as far from here as San Francisco is from, say, Denver."

"Well, maybe a long weekend then. A very long weekend."

The back door creaked open and Harry joined them. "Anyone up for another coffee? Herbal tea?"

Tess checked her watch. It was getting late and she had to be up early. And she needed to stop staring into Connor's eyes. "Tell her thanks, but no thanks. I should probably be heading off."

"Me too," Connor said, and he and Tess followed Harry back inside.

"We should do this again," Isabella announced. "It's been great!"

"Thanks so much for having me, Isabella, Harry. Dinner was fantastic."

As the men headed out the door, there was a hand on Tess's arm holding her back.

Isabella whispered. "He's cute. And available."

"I'm not interested. I'm here for wine not men."

"You sure?"

"Totally sure."

"What a pity."

It was a pity that her sister-in-law's attempt at match-making was lost on Tess. He was a hot guy who was, mysteriously, single. If there was a story there, Tess decided in that moment that she didn't want to know about it. In her experience, hot guys in small towns didn't stay single long.

In the distance, Connor and Harry shook hands, then looked back up to the house. Isabella sighed as she caught sight of her husband. Tess rolled her eyes.

Connor lifted his shades and looked across at Tess. Not Isabella, but directly at Tess. He'd been smiling and laughing with Harry but his expression had changed, become more serious. Even from this distance, she could see his smile had gone. And even from this distance, his gaze sent shivers right through her.

"I've got a plan for my life, Isabella, full of big ambitions. And the guys I meet? They haven't been able to cope with a woman who has big dreams of her own. They've always wanted me to change, to be *their* perfect woman. So, you

know what? I'm hanging out for the perfect guy for me."
Her voice dropped to a whisper. "So I figure I'm in for a
really long wait."

Isabella leaned in, spoke quietly in her sister-in-law's ear.
"No one's perfect, Tess. You're going to be waiting a hell of a
long time if you think such a man exists. I love your brother
with everything I have, but we still drive each other crazy
sometimes. And you know what I think? Perfect is pretty
damn boring."

As Connor drove away, the pulse in Tess's throat took a
long time to settle.

Something told her Connor Hawker wasn't boring.

Which was a sign that he wasn't the perfect guy.

And that was a very good sign indeed.

Chapter Eight

THERE WAS ALMOST no place Tess would rather be than in a vineyard.

Sure, the attractions of a day spa couldn't be overlooked, nor could the palm-fringed sandy beaches of Hawaii with their magical pink-and-orange sunsets. And sometimes, the comfort of her bed with a stack of pillows and a novel was a hard pull to resist.

But if she had to name her top ten, being out in the open air, surrounded by lines of vines as far as they eye could see until the distant perspective made them all a shimmering haze, would be number one with a bullet. She had grown up on the Harrison family property, which was a sprawling family estate with a number of smaller homes that had once been inhabited by workers, all surrounded by acres and acres of vineyards. Since it had been built, the winery had expanded and now there were holdings right throughout Napa Valley, but the original vines remained and their grapes made their way into some of Harrison's most renowned wines. During her childhood, the rhythms of life in the Harrison household had been dictated by the growing, pruning and picking seasons. And from her late teens, when she'd managed to convince her father that she too wanted to join the family business, to follow in his footsteps as the next winemaker in the Harrison dynasty, she'd been schooled in every aspect of it. She respected the history, the century-old vines, the soil, the geography and the heritage that had endured for generations.

But she wanted something else for her life. She wanted to build on the past, but also create a new and exciting future, and it was that desire that had brought her to Australia, to Wirralong and to this little patch of Matthews Wines. She was now in the middle of it, her steel-capped boots kicking up the red dust as she walked between rows of vines, her mind whirring at the inspiration in every step and at possibilities of what she might create back home.

Tess took off her wide-brimmed hat, lifted a forearm to wipe the sweat from her brow and then used the hat to swat the flies buzzing around her face. She gazed across to the horizon and took everything in. Up close, she was surrounded by plump stems and fresh green leaves, climbing tendrils and bunches of grapes hidden amongst them. In the middle distance, there was the lush scent of earth and promise and, in the distance, a blur of green and the wide blue sky opening up to forever.

There was something elemental about the seasons of a vineyard that she loved. She knew the season was about to turn by the new shoots or the fading of the colour of the leaf drop. This really was her idea of heaven.

She stopped to search amongst the leaves and bent to bury her face in the lushness. When she was a child, she and her sister Amy had pretended they were animals. Amy had always wanted to be an eagle, but Tess had always wanted to be a dog. Specifically a winery dog, so she could crawl right under the canopy of leaves and bunches and lie in the shade of these most precious plants.

Tess closed her eyes to luxuriate in the quiet, to listen to the rustle of the breeze in the vines. When she opened them she spotted someone walking toward her, carrying two buckets in one hand and a spade in the other. She knew instantly it was Connor. And so did her hormones. There were goose bumps on her arms that had nothing to do with feeling cold.

She'd found herself further into the middle of the vineyard than she'd expected, but she hadn't been planning on running into him.

When he realised it was her, he dipped his head a little and seemed to study the soil underfoot. She sucked in a deep breath and tried not to feel lightheaded. But it was Connor and she couldn't seem to control how her body reacted to him. All she could do was let it wash over her like a breeze.

"Hey," she called out and lifted a hand in a wave.

He was close before he responded, close enough that she could see that the damp patches on his high-viz shirt made it cling tight to him, over the strength of his shoulders, the curve of his chest and the sweep of his flat stomach. His face was in shade under the brim of his hat, but when he was at arms-length away he lifted his chin and flashed her a smile. "What are you doing out here?" he asked.

"Exploring," she replied, ignoring the quivering low in her stomach. There was no one else around. Just her and him and the seductive rustle of the leaves all around them, like the gentle lap of water on a quiet beach somewhere. "Toby told me all about how he converted this whole vineyard to organic four years ago and I wanted to come and see it for myself."

Connor put down the buckets and leaned the spade against one of the fence posts in the line of vines. He slipped off his aviator shades and lifted the corner of his shirt to wipe the sweat from his face. Tess copped an eyeful of muscle and stomach and pec and *oh my God* how she wanted to put her fingers there and trace his abs.

He propped his hands on his hips. "You used to this heat?"

She looked him up and down. "You think I'm wilting or something?" He wasn't wilting, in fact he seemed taller than he'd ever been. Sweat glistened on his forearms where he'd pushed up his sleeves. The growth on his jaw made him look slightly wild, as if he'd been living out here in the vineyard for days, with his bucket and his spade, digging for treasure. He looked to be completely in his element.

He took a step closer, peered at her face. "Your face is

red. Look out you don't get burnt. The sun here at Wirralong is strong." He slipped his glasses back on, shielding
what she saw there in his gaze, putting a shutter over what
she'd seen just then in his eyes. A flare. An unmistakeable
interest.

She patted the top of her hat. "That's what this is for.
Harry gave me the drill when I arrived at Matthews." Tess
dropped her voice to imitate her brother. "He's always
saying, 'No one wants you getting sunstroke, Brat.' As if I
would," she snorted.

Connor gazed at her and a flicker of a smile curved his
gorgeous mouth. "Brat?"

Her childhood nickname took on a whole new meaning
when Connor said it, drawled out slowly with a tease in his
tone, as if he was asking her to explain the bad behaviour
usually associated with such an epithet.

"Blame Harry. I do. I plan on getting my revenge one
day when he's too old and decrepit to chase me." She
nodded to the buckets. "What are you doing?"

"Soil tests."

She looked into them. One was empty; the other con-
tained ziplock plastic bags half-filled with soil samples.

"You looking for traces of synthetic chemicals or fertilis-
ers? There shouldn't be any if this is organic, right?"

"There shouldn't be. Toby and his team had to go
through a strict process to be certified organic in the first
place, which they've had for a year now. But part of that

ongoing certification involves an annual audit for compliance. These samples will go off to the lab and I'll send the results to the ACO, Australian Certified Organic. They're the crowd who do the certification services."

"Are you also looking for moisture levels?"

"Yep," Connor replied. "I'm sure you know the drill, Tess. If there isn't enough moisture in the soil, you'll get water stress in the vines. Which means reduced growth and—"

"—lower yields and poorer quality fruit," she finished his sentence for him. "And I also know that if Wirralong gets too much rain, there's a chance of diseases like downy mildew, right?"

Connor harrumphed. "Not that I think that's likely this winter. I've looked at the reports and last winter was dry and the long-term weather forecast is for much the same this year. It's getting dryer and dryer. Not only is the science irrefutable, but I see it with my own eyes."

His gorgeous eyes. She wanted to reach up to his face and whip off those damn shades so she could see them properly. Were his eyes bluer than the sky? Then she would run a finger down his cheek, over the curve of his jaw and the prickle of his stubble and slide it into his mouth.

"We've had drought in California, too. And terrible fires."

"I heard about those," Connor said. "We call them bushfires. You guys call them wildfires, right?"

"Wild, yeah."

"We have something in common." He paused. "My country and yours, I mean."

"We do."

"So," Tess started, not wanting the conversation to end. "Your job is to look after all the irrigation systems?"

He nodded. "And more. I monitor soil moisture, nutrition and the health of the vineyard. Keep all the records. I work alongside the winemaker to keep an eye on vine growth during the growing season. I deal with the agronomists and the lab. And," he stepped forward and adjusted her hat. "It's also my job to look after work health and safety on the vineyard and in the winery. Don't tip it back so much. Make sure you shade your face."

He lingered for a long moment, watching her.

"Yes, Boss," she said and saluted with a grin. "This is where I like to be, out here, not stuck behind a desk."

"Another thing we have in common. I have to be out here in the fresh air, to roll the soil between my fingertips. Smell it."

He crouched down and swept up a handful of earth from the stem of a vine. "Here."

Tess got to her knees. The two of them were in the shade of the canopy, hidden in a space that when she was a child she thought of as her cubby house. It was quieter here, intimate, just the two of them in their own little world.

"Hold out your hand," he said, and his voice was an invitation she couldn't refuse. She held out a hand. He cupped his left hand underneath hers, tugging her slightly closer to him. With his right, he drizzled a thin line of soil into her palm, slowly, like sand through an hourglass. It was cool and moist and she cupped her fingers to press them into her palm. Particles found their way into the creases of her skin. Her head line. Her heart line. Her life line. Her fate line.

His grip on her hand tightened and her bare knees pressed deeper into the cool soil as he pulled her closer. She put a hand on his knee to balance herself. His muscles moved and tightened under her touch.

"I'm about to fall," she said.

"I'd catch you."

She blew out a breath. Leaned back on her haunches. Studied his face. He was the work health and safety guy around here. Of course he would catch her. Of course he wouldn't let anything happen to her.

He stood up, reached a hand down to her and pulled her to her feet. They stood in silence for a long moment.

Finally, he spoke. "If you've got nothing on, I could do with a hand finishing these samples."

Tess considered her options. A slow walk back to her desk to finish her proposal for the board of Harrison's Wines. Or spend the rest of the afternoon with Connor in the vineyard. There was no choice, really.

"Hand me that spade."

Chapter Nine

AFTER WORK THAT night, Connor gripped the cricket bat between his hands and stared down the pitch in the practice nets while Eddie lurched toward him, winding up and bringing his arm over. The ball dawdled down the pitch and Connor stopped it in its tracks with a blocking shot. He didn't have the heart to belt it past the bloke, so he gave it a little bit of a push and it bounced three times before Eddie scooped it up.

He would never trouble any batter, that was for sure.

"You want another over?" Eddie called eagerly.

"Thanks, mate, but I think I'm done." He tucked his cricket bat under an arm and tugged off his padded gloves. He reached out to Eddie and the men shook hands.

"We appreciate you joining the team." Eddie tossed the ball from palm to palm, as if he were juggling. "It's a real shame you missed the first few games of the season. We got thumped by nearly every team in the region. We're a bit desperate for someone who can bat."

"I'll do my best, but I'm a bit rusty. I haven't played for a while. For a few years, to be honest."

Eddie chuckled. "It didn't show. I know you were going easy on me. I could see you were holding back. You've got a cover drive that'll come in bloody handy this Saturday afternoon when we play Arthurton. They're animals!"

The Arthurton Animals. Good name for a team, Connor thought as he smiled at Eddie's infectious enthusiasm. "We'll see. If they bowl anything like you, I'll be hitting them into the car park."

Eddie laughed and slapped his knee. "Mate, anyone who hits a six gets a free beer at the club."

"So, we're playing home on Saturday, right?" Connor asked.

"Sure are. See you at ten o'clock for a warm up."

Connor shook Eddie's hand in farewell. "See you there." He unstrapped his protective cricket pads, stowed them with his gloves and helmet in his sports bag and headed to his car. He'd been hoping a good batting session would release some of the tension that had been hardening inside him since the dinner last night at Harry and Isabella's. It had been four days since he'd met her, and Tess was so far inside his head that he was even dreaming about her.

Yeah, the kind of dreams you had when you haven't had sex with anyone in a whole goddamn year. The kind of dreams that mean you're more exhausted when you wake up than when you fall asleep, which was not good. He'd come to practice tonight burning with a desire to take all that pent-up sexual energy—frustration more like it—and whack the hell out of the cricket ball, to send it soaring into the blue summer sky over the tops of the gum trees that ringed the oval. But he couldn't do that with Eddie's half-assed bowling, and he hadn't wanted to embarrass the guy. He'd need to go running instead, pound the wide streets of Wirralong for an hour in a big loop to untie the knot.

He drove back into town and tried to think about cricket. About work. About underground irrigation lines and rainfall and the weather forecast and every other single thing that came second nature to him.

But she was still there.

Music filled the cabin of his four-wheel drive and he cranked up the volume. If he had a dog, he would have wound the window right down and let the mutt stick its head out into the wind, eyes squinting in pleasure, tongue flapping in the wind. That's what he needed to do, although maybe without the tongue flapping. He unwound his window, stuck his head out into the rush of the slipstream to see if it would sweep every thought about her from his mind.

Two minutes. Five minutes maybe.

Twenty minutes later, when he slammed the car door and stomped up the stairs to his apartment in Wirralong's main street, thrust the key in the lock, strode through the sparsely furnished living room—a leather sofa, a wide screen TV and a coffee table—and went straight into the shower, she was still there.

As he stripped off his sweaty cricket gear and dropped it

on the floor, as he sudsed himself in the shower, hot water loosening his tight shoulders, soap drizzling down his body and making the tiles underfoot slick, she was fucking well still there.

He cranked off the hot water and stood in the cold spray for a few minutes.

That didn't help either.

He dressed, poured himself a glass of wine and flopped back on to the leather sofa. Lifted his bare feet to rest on the footstool that matched the sofa. He flicked on the TV and flicked channels aimlessly. Surely there might be a day-night cricket match he could watch to take his mind off wanting her.

It had only been four freaking days, during which he'd lost his mind. He wanted her like he hadn't wanted anyone for a long, long time. He wanted to get her naked, to feel every part of her under him, to caress her skin and make her quiver in his arms. Hell yes, he wanted the rush of release for himself, but he wanted to see her eyes squint close and her mouth fall open as she came under his fingers.

But he shouldn't want it. He couldn't want her.

She was a Harrison and he worked for the Harrisons now. It was never a good idea to mix that kind of business with that kind of pleasure. He'd made that mistake once before and he'd ended up alone at the altar.

And anyway, she was from somewhere else and was going back there in a few weeks. If he needed anyone, it had to be someone who'd stick around. Who wanted the house and the life here in Australia, and the dog.

Especially the dog.

He jabbed the remote control at the TV and the screen went black. There was an ache in his lower back that nagged. He should have warmed up before playing cricket tonight. He should have prepared himself better to ward off an injury.

And when it came to Tess, he'd better take that same advice. He'd better prepare himself for tomorrow, when he was going to work with her all day. He needed his strength to fight off the almost uncontrollable urge to ask her out to dinner.

And then get her naked.

Chapter Ten

THE SMART LADIES Supper Club ritually gathered once a fortnight, and tonight Maggie was the host. Tess had had a long week surrounded by men—Harry, Toby and now the distractingly sexy and totally off-limits Connor Hawker—and she was looking forward to the company of her friends.

In many ways, the women reminded Tess of the girls she'd gone to college with. They'd been young women from all over the world—almost every continent in fact. They'd been tight as you could be, but since graduating they'd returned to their home countries and many weren't even making wine for a living. And yes, while there was Facebook and Skype and WhatsApp and Insta, those apps couldn't make up for the kind of friendship she had found in Wirralong, the face-to-face camaraderie she could see right in front of her eyes. Tess herself had been welcomed with warmth and open arms and they'd made a deal: as long as Tess brought the wine, the others would supply all the cheese and crackers and olives and pâté they could eat. It was a sweet deal.

The sun was setting and it cast long shadows over the manicured lawns of Wirra Station. Tomorrow, there would be another wedding and Maggie would work her magic with her team and Isabella would undertake the marriage officiant duties and dutifully join two people in matrimony. Tess would assume her position on her porch and mock, of course. But tonight, all was relatively quiet at Maggie's property. Max was working in his office upstairs and the Smart Ladies were lounging around Maggie's expansive living room, their bare feet elevated on Moroccan leather ottomans, their glasses filled, and their conversation lively.

They really were wonderful women and had been so welcoming to both Isabella and Tess. They were all about the same age, give or take a couple of years, and had all found themselves in Wirralong. Under Maggie's guidance and sure hand, Wirra Station was fast becoming one of the premier wedding and event destinations in regional Victoria. Tess knew there had been some recent glowing reviews in a whole host of wedding magazines, and some of the most popular wedding bloggers had featured photos of the magnificent grounds and the historic stone Woolshed. That had been the lightning that had lit the spark of interest and the venue was booked up for almost the next two years. Maggie had taken a risk when she'd restored the homestead, and it was paying off in spades.

Tess's thoughts drifted back to the raucous conversation going on all around her.

"So she insisted on the purple, even though I tried to politely suggest something a little more subtle might suit her," Elsa laughed. "But then I thought ... you know what? Why can't you have bright purple hair when you're eighty-five?"

Serenity flicked at her bottle orange hair, so bright it was almost fluorescent. "Hear, hear. Life's too short, I reckon. Live a little."

"Exactly," Maggie added. "We should always use the good dinner settings."

"And travel halfway across the world and fall in love!" Emmaline proclaimed.

"Or travel halfway across the world and get married in Vegas!" Maggie announced with a wink at Isabella.

Isabella had the grace to blush. "Not that I would recommend doing the whole runaway bride thing, but it worked out in the end. It worked out very well, in fact."

There was too much gushy talk about falling in love for Tess's liking, which seemed to layer on top of Isabella's concerted attempts to set up Tess with Connor. She thought about their conversation out in the vineyard yesterday. The way their fingers had touched. The look in his eyes. The way she'd imagined him naked.

She quickly changed the subject.

"And drink all the wine!" she called out, which caused a rousing cheer.

Serenity leaned forward and turned her attention to Isabella. "Who are you marrying tomorrow, Iz? What's the romantic story behind the couple? I'm dying to know."

Please God not another romantic story, Tess thought to herself.

Isabella took a deep breath. "Well," she began.

As Isabella told the tale of Meryl and Jason and how they'd met, Tess turned toward Maggie sitting to her left.

"Hey, Maggie. I've been meaning to talk to you about your wine supplier."

Maggie raised an eyebrow and her glass. "I'm listening."

"I know I haven't been here all that long, but I like making lists and crossing things off. It's a thing I do. And one of those things is to put a deal to you."

"Still listening."

"How would you feel about Matthews being the exclusive supplier of organic wine for your events here at Wirra Station?"

Maggie cocked her head. "Interesting. This place came with a cellar full of some fantastic vintage bottles, which we pull out for very special occasions, but not every bride and groom have the budget for those top end wines. What are you thinking?"

"I'm sure we could do a really good price for you. And the fact that it's an organic range might be a great selling point for some of your guests. Can't you just see it? Young couples looking for the perfect wedding in the perfect wedding venue in this stunning bushland setting, with the trees whispering all around them and the birdsong and the setting sun, as if they're at one with nature. Organic wines just seem like the perfect fit for people so dedicated to getting married in a place like this."

Tess was suddenly aware that the noise all around them had ceased. Tess was aware she had a tendency to make speeches and wasn't sure if they all found it a bit, well, American.

"Oh my God," Isabella sighed. "That's perfect."

"You think so?" Tess looked over at her sister-in-law.

Maggie sat forward in her leather sofa. Her eyes were wide and bright. "We've grown so fast I've hardly had time to do much, but that's a brilliant idea. It really suits our brand. I've also been planning to talk to the two women who own the bush tucker business in the main street. They're just getting off the ground and I know they're scouting around for suppliers and they're working with people in the community. What do you all think? What if they could start catering some of our events? It would be a help to them and to us. The total Wirralong experience, right? Local organic wine courtesy of Matthews. Local food, too."

Tess looked at each of the Smart Ladies. "Bush tucker? Is that like a country picnic or something?"

"It's the name for the plants and foods traditionally eaten by local Aboriginal people," Maggie explained. "And it's not just kangaroo, which is what everyone thinks of at first, but there are some incredible fruits, nuts, seeds and different plants. Bush tomatoes. Native pears and cucumbers. Have you ever tasted a finger lime? It's a citrusy taste explosion in your mouth."

"That sounds incredible," said Tess. "And a real point of difference for Wirra Station."

Maggie beamed at her. "You do have a business brain, don't you?"

Tess lapped up the praise. She was never credited with thinking like that in the competitive environment of her own family, that was for sure, which had piled on the pressure for the plan she was going to put to the Board. Would they take her proposal seriously? Inside, she had a quaking fear that they would always think of her as the flaky young winemaker who only cared about the wine and not carrying on the legacy of the Harrison family enterprise. Maggie's words had bolstered Tess's confidence no end and she fought back the urge to lean over and give Maggie a hug.

"Don't you have a mini-conference here in April?" Emmaline asked as she sliced a wedge of camembert from the round in the middle of the fruit platter on the coffee table. "The state's physiotherapists association or some such?"

Maggie laughed at Emmaline. "How on earth do you consistently keep coming up with incredible ideas? You're like an energiser bunny, Lady E."

Emmaline shrugged and smiled. "It's that English can-do attitude, I expect."

"And I love it."

"What about starting off with a tasting?" Elsa added, her curious eyes wide. "Some canapes and an exclusive event here at Wirra Station? We could invite the Mayor and some food and wine bloggers. You could set up the tasting table under the gums outside, Tess. It's stunning there in the afternoon."

Tess flopped back on the sofa. Her cheeks were hot and her head was buzzing with excitement. *Yes, yes, yes.* She could take everything she'd learned here and expand on it back home. Wait until she told Harry about the possibility of becoming the exclusive supplier to Wirra Station for weddings and events.

And the idea of tastings blossomed in her imagination, too. The gorgeous little stone cottage out at the winery was beautiful but small. The grounds of Wirra were rolling and lush and there was room in the cellar to store cases of wine for sale. And if that worked well, she could suggest establishing a shopfront tasting room in the main street of Wirralong. If Wirra Station was busy with functions, the people who were coming to Wirralong were a captive audience who might not necessarily have the time to drive out to the winery.

Oh yes. This was exactly how a small winery like Matthews could make its presence felt, could find a space—even a little one—alongside the corporate brands and major international producers. Not to mention all the other plans she was thinking about: to fully introduce biodynamic principles to the winery; to divert waste from landfill; to, all in all, do better for the environment.

She couldn't wait to tell Connor.

Harry. She meant Harry, of course.

Chapter Eleven

ISABELLA MARTENSON WAS a smart and conniving woman.

So smart and conniving that she'd somehow managed to convince Tess to pack a picnic lunch, two bottles of wine and a folding chair and set herself up under the shade of the swaying gum trees that ringed the Wirralong Oval to watch ... *cricket*. And Isabella was so smart and conniving that she'd managed to get Wirralong's two resident Americans—Tess and Harry—to watch this most non-American of games. Without her.

"Cheers," Harry said as he clinked glasses with Tess.

"I can't believe I'm here. This was all Isabella's idea and where is she? Off marrying someone. Your wife is really determined to make you an Aussie, isn't she? And you are letting it happen, bit by bit. Soon you'll be sounding like that crocodile guy."

Harry looked out across the oval with great concentration. "She hasn't had to work too hard, I have to admit. I think she wants to make sure that if we have kids, we'll stay here and raise them as little Aussie vegemites. That's what she says. *Little Aussie vegemites*. It's cute, right? You wait, Brat. Once you've hung around long enough, this place sure works its magic on you. And so will this weird-ass game."

Tess clucked her tongue. "What was that quote that Dad used to repeat when Mom told him to get a hobby? That *golf is a good walk ruined*? I'm beginning to think that cricket is a good picnic ruined."

"Listen, Tess." Harry leaned forward in his chair, a cheeky grin on his face. "Don't let on to Isabella, but I don't have a clue about this game, either. And I'm fully aware that I might not ever understand it. But what I know, and what I know she loves about it, is that it's about slowing down. Sitting here under the trees. Smelling the eucalypts. Letting the breeze cool the sweat on your neck so you don't melt from these insane Australian summer temperatures. There's something kind of … I don't know … therapeutic about listening to the crack of the ball on the bat as the guy out there whacks it into the trees at the other end. About the long periods of waiting while nothing actually happens, the beers at lunch, the amazing country catering for afternoon tea and the conversation and camaraderie."

Tess studied the peaceful look on her brother's face. "Oh my God. Harry. You've joined a cult, haven't you?"

"What?"

"Or maybe the local tourist bureau or something? The Wirralong Progress Association? Is there even such a thing? Wait until I tell Amy and Everett about this. Boy, oh, boy.

Mr all-American is turning into an Aussie. They won't believe it."

Harry laughed heartily. "They both loved Wirralong when they came for the wedding, if you remember. And just you wait. This place will suck you right in before you know it."

Tess leaned back in her chair and crossed her arms adamantly. "That will not happen. This is nothing but a pit stop, another line on my CV, Bro."

They both turned toward the players at the sound of a raucous "Howzat!" from the bowler. The stooped umpire raised his hand and held up a single finger. The players who'd been scattered all over the ground—the fielders?—rushed to the bowler guy and there was some kind of group hug before all the players left the field.

"They must be all out," Harry said. "The Wirralong Bushrangers will be batting now."

A few minutes later, Tess and Harry watched the two Bushrangers opening batters take to the field. The goose bumps on the back of her neck announced to Tess that one of them was Connor. There was something about his long-legged stride that she already recognised. His uniform and shoes were white and caught the early afternoon sun, reflecting so bright they appeared as if they'd just been bleached. The helmet he held in his hand was dark green and Tess found herself watching with intense and focused interest as he stripped off his padded gloves and tightened the helmet's strap under his chin. The clothes were loose, no surprise given the heat, but they couldn't disguise his broad shoulders, his muscular legs and the strength in his arms.

Damn it to hell. How was it even possible to feel prickles on her skin when she was mopping the sweat from her brow and fanning her face with her sunhat like a proper Southern belle? Connor had totally thrown her off her game and she'd been asking herself the same question over and over: why him?

"I just don't understand it," Tess muttered.

"Oh, you will," Harry replied.

"Huh?" She snapped back to the game.

"You'll understand cricket before you know it. So Iz keeps telling me."

Tess didn't correct her brother. She wasn't talking about sport. She was talking about the biological reaction, the pure physical attraction, that pinged inside her whenever she was in close proximity to Connor. It was as if all her hormones were standing at attention, on high alert for just him, and whenever they got a whiff of his pheromones, or whatever they were, they started cavorting traitorously in a happy rumba in her ovaries.

Whatever was between them had to sizzle and die out. Didn't it?

"Bro, if you and Iz have kids ... do you think you'll ever come home?"

He turned to her, lifted his sunglasses and pushed them

back on his hair. "You mean to Napa?"

Tess nodded. She and Harry had always been close and the thought that he would forever be here on the other side of the world felt like one of her limbs was missing. They'd already lost their mother. Their father was still hale and hearty, but he wouldn't be forever. All she had left were Harry and Amy and Everett. It felt to her as if, one by one, her family was drifting apart. Thanksgiving at Amy's house would never be the same, nor would Christmas dinner at her father's, with Harry so far away. Families were bound by fragile threads and if they were stretched too far, she was sure they would snap like a crusty elastic band.

Harry searched Tess's face. With a gentle movement, he rested his hand on her forearm. "Don't worry, Tess. Family is family."

"It's just that … Wirralong is so far away, Harry."

"What's a few time zones? I've found her, Tess, and I'd follow that woman to the four corners of the earth." He chuckled. "As a matter of fact, I did."

She covered her brother's hand with her own and gave it a squeeze. "She drove you a bit crazy, Bro."

"The best ones do, Brat."

Out in the middle of the oval, Connor's big padded glove was hovering over his crotch. And then he pushed at his trousers and rearranged himself. Tess's cheeks began to burn. Just how big was his package that it got in the way? "What the …?"

"He's adjusting his box," Harry explained, noting her intense interest.

Tess swallowed the sudden lump in her throat. "I've never heard it called that before."

Harry playfully bumped her shoulder with his. "His protection, you idiot. No guy wants to be hit there. Ever." He paused. "You thinking about his—"

"No. Definitely not. Shut up right now."

"What's the harm, Tess? Have some fun. He's single. He's a great guy as far as I can tell and I can't remember the last time you actually mentioned a guy."

"That's because I'm a very wise woman who doesn't tell her brother everything about her love life."

"So you have a love life?"

"I'm your sister, not a nun. And anyway, we work together. In the same actual office. It would be monumentally stupid."

And monumentally hot. Because Connor was just about the sexiest guy she'd met in a long, long time. Maybe ever. Hotter than her first, second and third boyfriends combined, with daylight in between.

"So you are interested."

Tess squinted into the distance, trying to make out Connor's features. It was hard to see anything behind the peak on the top of his helmet and the grill that wrapped around his face. But there was no mistaking the wide and strong shoulders, the flat planes of his stomach and his long, long legs.

Her treacherous pulse thudded at seeing him. "I. Am. Not. Interested. In. The. Slightest."

"You said it yourself, Brat. You're going home. Live a little."

The bowler ran in and Connor swung at the ball, striking it with a hard crack. It flew through the air and into the scrub on the far side of the oval. People all around clapped and cheered. Automatically, Tess joined in.

Connor raised his bat in the air to acknowledge the applause. He lifted his helmet from his head, wiped the sweat from his brow with his forearm and she could have sworn he looked directly at her and smiled.

At least her dancing hormones thought so.

HOURS LATER, TESS didn't want to admit that Connor and Isabella were kind of right about this peculiar game. Sure, she could have been on her porch watching the wedding Isabella had officiated, but sitting in the shade and watching the confusing coming and goings was actually turning out to be quite a leisurely pastime. The hours went by quickly, helped by the food she'd packed and the couple of glasses of wine she'd sipped until she'd started on the soda water. She'd snuck a novel in her picnic basket and felt no guilt about dipping in and out of the pages when a cheer went up, when she needed to distract herself from watching Connor. When he hit his fiftieth run, there was a rousing standing ovation from the crowd and the rest of his team waiting in a cluster around a picnic table laden with snacks and tubs filled with ice and beers.

Isabella arrived by late afternoon and headed straight to Harry for a kiss.

"Husband," she said lovingly.

"Wife," Harry replied.

"Hey, Tess."

"Hey, Iz. How was the wedding?"

"Beautiful. Everyone cried. The sun shone just at the right moment. And the flower girl threw up in the rose bushes. Enjoying the game?"

"Game? What game? I've been too busy reading my novel to notice."

"Don't believe a word of it," Harry said. "She's been transfixed the whole time."

"Have not."

"Have too."

Isabella laughed. "They're coming off for tea break. My timing is perfect. Oh look, here comes Connor."

Tess's hormones knew it before Isabella announced it. She pushed her sunglasses back up her nose so Connor wouldn't see the lust that she was sure was radiating from her eyes like Cyclops in the *X-Men* movies. She grabbed her novel for protection and tried to find the last sentence she'd read. The words swam.

"Connor," Isabella called out. "What's the score?"

Connor replied with an answer filled with numbers that made no sense to Tess.

"Hey, Harry," Connor said.

"Looks like you're holding on out there. You hit a fifty. That's good right?"

Out of the corner of her eye, Tess saw Connor shift his weight from one leg to the other, cock his hip. The ridiculous padded leg things he was wearing looked like armour, but softer.

"I've hit better, but it's all right. The other team are struggling for bowlers, which makes it easy for me." He paused. "Hi, Tess."

"Hey, Connor." She glanced up to his face for a quick smile and then returned her attention to her book. Nothing sank into her swooning head.

"Good book?"

She flipped it over to look at the cover, as if she needed reminding about what she was reading. "Yeah. Sure. It's the latest Liane Moriarty. You know what they say. When in Rome …"

Connor pushed his sunglasses to the top of his head. "Thanks for coming out, being part of the cheer squad." He smiled and looked her right in the eyes. Oh God, it was warm and genuine and perfect.

Oh no. No no no no.

"Well. I had nothing better to do."

He cocked an eyebrow at her. "No weddings to watch today?"

She craned her neck to meet his gaze. Blue eyes. A sheen of sweat on his brow. Oh my. With a quick glance to her right, Tess realised that Harry and Isabella were deep in a conversation of their own.

"Oh, that's hilarious. You're really funny, you know that? I don't watch the weddings, no matter what you might think. That day you saw me, I just happened to be sitting out on my front porch enjoying the cool afternoon breeze. I'm an outdoors gal. I work outside. I hate being stuck in an office or in my living room. Last time I looked this was a free country."

She lifted her eyes to his. There was a dare flashing between them. He leaned down. His gaze dropped to her lips and she broke out in a sweat.

"You free for dinner tonight?" His voice was like aged whiskey and it had the same effect on her. Heat coursed down her throat and into her belly.

"Dinner."

"I haven't been to Janu's in the main street. I hear it's pretty amazing."

"I've heard that, too. It's got a great wine list, apparently. The best of French, Italian, New Zealand and they even stock American wine. Who would have thought?"

The rumba in her ovaries rumbled lower, and those hormones were now doing triple flips.

"Eight good for you?"

Her eyes travelled past his mouth, the brown skin of his neck, over his pecs where the damp fabric of his uniform had shrunk to fit like cling wrap in a microwave.

You're going home soon.

He's cute and available.

Live a little.

"Sure. Why not. A gal's gotta eat, right?"

His lips curved in a smile. "I'll pick you up about seven thirty."

"Great."

And as Connor strode over to his team mates, he looked over his shoulder at her and saw she was watching him walk away. He dipped his head and continued on.

Tess dropped the novel in her lap.

Oh no no no no no.

Chapter Twelve

CONNOR HAWKER HAD always known how to perform under pressure. When he'd played cricket at school, and later on at local clubs as he'd grown older, he could always be relied upon to score the runs when his team needed them.

At work, he performed best when the pressure was on. When vineyard owners and winemakers were on his back, worried about their multimillion-dollar investments, he could hold his own in all those debates.

And when his fiancée had called to tell him she wasn't turning up to their wedding, he'd calmly walked into the old stone church and announced to the guests that the wedding was off. He'd encouraged them to stay and have a drink and eat all the food that was already paid for, and he'd held it together to have a couple of beers himself, and let his family and friends commiserate and share their shock with him. Just because his day—and his life—had been ruined, it didn't mean they couldn't have a feed.

It hadn't been until later that he'd fallen apart. He'd made it through the afternoon in some kind of shock, numbness reaching into every limb and his heart and his head as he tried to take it all in. He'd booked tickets for a honeymoon, a surprise trip to Bali for him and Juliette. He'd had to cancel it. In the solitude of his hotel room with an array of opened and empty bottles from the mini-bar scattered on the floor, he'd let the emotions he'd been holding on to pour from him like water from a burst dam.

And then it was done.

He'd never spoken about it after that.

And he'd vowed to never again let himself get so lost in someone else.

He'd packed up his house—the home he'd bought before he'd met Juliette and had been planning to make their marital home—and rented it out. The rent money gave him some time to do a road trip up to the Hunter Valley to see some old mates, to decompress, to clear her out of his head. Only later would he realise that it would take more than a long drive over the Hay plain. Then, he'd driven all the way back home and got back to work. But nothing could hold him. Home had too many memories clawing away at his peace of mind, so he kept moving. And then when the next place began feeling too comfortable, he up and moved again. And then again. He hadn't wanted to settle anywhere, because any place that started to feel like home opened up the jagged wound again, made him think about what a home was, what it should be. It should be a place filled with someone special to share it with and all that meant. A place of comfort. A comfortable sofa at the end of the day. Sex. Lots of sex. Jokes. A dog. And most important of all, love. And someone who loved you back.

Love had just hurt, gnawed at him like a jagged scar, and he didn't want to feel that way ever again.

But lust?

He could do that. He needed to satisfy that craving. And man, oh man, was he having lustful thoughts about Tess. Since that first day when he'd walked into the tasting room at Matthews Wines, something had zinged in the air between them, something indefinable, something completely against his will. He didn't want to feel it for her, especially, a colleague. But it was something he needed, that was for damn sure.

And judging by the way she'd been looking at him— yeah, he'd noticed—maybe, just maybe, she needed it too. Did she have someone back in America? He didn't think so. She talked a lot about her family, her father Charles, and Harry and—who were the others? Everett and Amy? He could tell when they were on the other end of the line. Her face lit up. Her voice lifted, became light and breezy and happy, and the back and forth banter made him smile even though he wasn't supposed to be listening in to someone else's phone conversation.

He hadn't noticed any phone calls that had elicited a soft tone in her voice, an intimate expression, a need for some privacy.

Good. Because he was on his way to her place to pick her up for a dinner and he was hoping that might lead to something else. He had to give in to the need, the craving he had to feel a woman's body, to kiss her soft lips, to lose himself in her.

That afternoon, while he'd been out batting, he'd felt her eyes on him. And go on, call him a macho idiot, but knowing that she was watching had made him try harder. He'd batted with more aggression. He'd run faster between the wickets. And none of that was about impressing Eddie and the rest of the blokes in the team. Damn it, he had one aim in mind and that was to impress the fuck out of Tess. When he'd hit his fifty and glanced over to the crowd of onlookers, he'd seen her leap out of her chair, clapping and whooping, calling his name, and he'd decided at that very moment that he had to do something about the tension sizzling between them.

There had to be some resolution to it or he would go crazy.

He pulled up at Wirra Station, right out front of Tess's little cottage, at seven thirty on the dot. It had been a hot day and although the sun was on its way into evening, it was still hot and humid. He'd chosen tan chinos and a pale white linen shirt, its sleeves folded to his elbows and the back of it felt a little damp from the ride over in the car. He didn't know why he was sweating when he'd had the air-conditioner going full bore in the cabin.

He knocked on the door and when Tess flung it open a moment or two later, he couldn't speak. Or breathe, suddenly. A loose white dress skimmed over her body and hit her legs just above the knee. The little straps across her shoulders revealed skin that looked like silk. She smelt like a rose garden and her blond hair curled at her shoulders, as if a breeze was blowing through the room just for her.

"Hey, Connor. Come in."

"Hi. These are for you." They were only a bunch of wildflowers that he'd gathered from around Wirralong Oval before he'd left earlier that afternoon, but he'd thought they might be new and exotic to Tess.

"Oh my God. Thank you." She lifted the bunch to her face, closed her eyes and sniffed deep and generously. Then she looked up at him with a beaming smile and it felt like the floor collapsed under him.

"They smell like lemons," she said with a sigh.

"They're wildflowers." He turned to her, suddenly conscious of how close she was, her scent, the brush of her shoulder against his arm as she moved. How beautiful she was.

"They're gorgeous. I'll put them in some water. Follow me." Tess closed the door behind him and swayed across the living room to the kitchen. "It's a lovely night. It's cooled down some. You must have been hot as hell out there today in the middle of the field."

"Oval."

"Field. Oval. Pitch. I don't really do sports. As you can probably tell, right? You're lucky I didn't call it a tennis court." She laughed and the sound was joyful and playful. "And I only know that because we have a tennis court at home. Not that I ever played tennis on it. I used to ride my bike around and around in there when I was a kid. And I've gotta tell you, that Astroturf stuff isn't as soft as it looks. Scratching yourself on that hurts like hell."

"Didn't know that." Connor watched every step of hers with intense concentration. He rubbed a palm over his bristly hair.

"We've got time for a glass of wine before we head to Janu's. Care for one?"

Man. Had she done that on purpose? Swung her hips like that? How come he'd never noticed the sway of her ass before, the casual, sexy stroll that flicked up the hem of her dress, as if she were twirling. She'd opened a bottle of red and when he could think straight, he noticed two gleaming glasses on the kitchen bench, along with two small bowls filled with olives and pretzels.

"Sure."

He heard the liquid splash of the wine as he looked around the room. There were no personal touches. No photographs or art works. Not even a pile of magazines on the coffee table. Just a TV, an old floral fabric sofa, a small dining table with two chairs. It looked temporary. He recognised that particular decorating approach.

He heard her footsteps and turned, took a step. Too quickly.

They were suddenly face-to-face. The two glasses Tess was holding were now pressed into his chest, their contents splashing in the air. Connor watched it as if it was playing in slow motion. Tess's mouth agape in horror, her eyes wide. The droplets of wine like falling rain. The cold soak of it into the fabric of his shirt. The splash pattern on her white dress like oil paint flicked on a canvas.

And then Tess sprung back to life. "Holy crap!" Her eyes lowering to the stain spreading on Connor's linen shirt. "I'm so, so sorry. I … damn it."

"It was my fault. I wasn't looking." *Your problem was you were looking too closely.* He pinched the fabric of his shirt and pulled it away from his chest. It was soaked.

Tess rushed to put the glasses back on the kitchen bench and then reached for his hand. "Come on, quick."

Her grip was firm and he let himself be led through the house to the laundry. There was a small silver tub, a washing machine and a dryer and a rail with a grey towel neatly draped over it.

She let go of his hand and her fingers scrambled to the buttons on his shirt. As she deftly slid them through the holes, she mumbled into his chest, "You know about red wine stains, right? We have to get this thing soaking as soon as possible. It's a nice shirt. I'd hate to think I ruined it. Oh my God, it's linen, too."

She undid another button and seemed to be getting slower. Was she trembling?

Her eyes darted to his and he felt her breath on the exposed skin of his chest.

"You wouldn't want it ruined because I'm a klutz."

He took a step closer. "I should be more careful."

His shirt was open now. Tess reached around his back and tugged the tails out of his chinos. Her breasts brushed against him and he had to hold back from groaning, and then she slowed, met his gaze. It was pure torture. Tess smoothed her hands up his chest, taking time to linger on his pecs and the curve of his shoulders, and she slipped her fingers in between his skin and the fabric before pushing it back off his shoulders. His arms were caught behind him in the tangle of his sleeves. He breathed deep as her fingers traced a scorching line down over his pecs to the muscles of his stomach. Suddenly he wasn't hungry for food, but for something much more satisfying, primal and essential. Skin on skin. Two people. Sex.

"What about your dress?" He meant the stain on it but once the words were whispered in the air between them, he wasn't sure anymore. There was a new pressure in her fingers on his skin and she pushed him. "Turn around."

He obeyed her. She pulled his shirt from his arms and it crumpled to the floor. He heard a zip unfasten and a rustle of fabric and then the splash of water in the laundry tub. When he slowly turned, Tess had wrapped herself in the grey towel and was tucking one end inside the top like women did. It covered her breasts but was barely long enough to cover her ass. He didn't see bra straps, only bare shoulders, and he took in every inch of that bare skin, letting himself imagine what was under that towel and how it would feel and taste.

He looked her up and down slowly. "Not sure what we're going to do now. The only spare shirt in my car is fluorescent yellow and covered in dirt."

"We'd better cancel, huh?" Tess bit her lip.

Connor nodded.

"Do you want to call the restaurant?" she murmured as she watched his mouth. "I could never show my face in Wirralong again if we bailed without at least a phone call."

"Sure." He pulled his phone from the pocket of his trousers, called Janu's and apologised. Tess hadn't moved. She was watching his mouth, and she was so close he could make out the flecks of amber in her eyes, could feel her breath on his chest.

Sweet Jesus.

He waited, needing to be certain he wasn't misreading the signs, needing to be sure she wanted this as much as he did.

"Tess. Tell me you want this. I need to hear you say it."

"I want this. I want you." She pressed her lips to his chest and licked him like he was a melting ice cream.

"I want this, too." He reached for a strand of her hair

and twisted its golden silkiness around his fingers. He didn't want to let go.

"And the thing is, I don't know why, exactly," Tess murmured. "You are so not my type."

"Flattery will get you everywhere." He felt his mouth curve into a wide grin and he liked how it felt. He liked how she made him feel.

"I mean it."

"Pity."

"Yeah. First," she poked a finger at his stomach. "I need a man who actually likes to talk. You know, like have an actual conversation."

As if to prove her point, he stared back at her for a long moment. "Talking is overrated."

"Second of all." Another jab with her finger as she glanced at up his hair. "I'd prefer someone who can actually be bothered to do more with his hair than get a buzz cut."

Without thinking, he ran a flat palm over it. "You don't like my hair?"

"Not particularly. But it's your hair. You can do whatever you like with it." He leaned down to kiss her pink, puffed, pursed lips. Hung back at the final moment to see if it would make her catch her breath. It did.

"Is there a number three?" Connor kissed her neck, tasted her, breathed her in.

Tess arched her neck to give him space. "Number three. My type … is a man who has a plan for his life, someone who sticks at something, thinks about his future."

"Thinking about the future is over-rated, Tess. Sometimes it's better thinking about the right here. The right now."

"And the whole working together thing doesn't bother you?" she asked.

"You told me yourself. You're only here for a few weeks." He moved his head; his lips were closer to hers now. She breathed deep and pressed her breasts into his chest. She was warm and so willing. And he was hungry for her. Could she feel him? He pressed his arousal into her belly and her breath caught.

"True," she breathed. "So, let me just be clear. What happens tonight has no bearing on tomorrow or the day after that or …"

"The day after that. What happens here tonight stays here, Tess."

He wanted her. He needed her. He needed her like vines needed water and sunshine if they were to thrive. In that moment, everything he knew about himself was thrown into the air like confetti at a wedding. Hadn't he vowed never to want a woman again?

He lifted a hand, grazed his fingers from her shoulder down past her elbow, over the goose bumps on her forearm, to her fingers.

She shivered. "Look. Just so you know. I haven't done this in a little while, Connor. I may go a little crazy. I may get … out of control."

"I fucking well hope so," he whispered into her ear.

She shivered and her fingers dug into his forearms. "You're so not my type, Connor Hawker."

"Thank fuck for that."

Chapter Thirteen

OH MY FREAKING God.

Connor Hawker was sexy and half-naked in front of her and his skin felt so smooth and he tasted so good. The sticky stain from the spilled red wine was a dark pink splatter on his tanned skin. She licked it, the taste of the wine mixed up with the taste of him. She should have taken more time to taste him, she should have been more patient. Because he looked that delicious.

But God, Tess wanted him as much as he wanted her and there was no time to waste. She really, really needed to have sex. With somebody. With anybody. It had been a long time. Twelve whole freaking months.

Thank God this wasn't perfect. Dates shouldn't start with spilled wine and stained clothes and an offer of sex in the goddamn laundry room. But that look in his eyes and the hitch in his breath had her gasping and desperate. She was totally up for no-strings-attached sex with a handsome Australian.

Tess stepped back from Connor and pulled the towel loose. It fell to the floor and she got so much satisfaction from watching him take her in, every inch of her. He swallowed hard, his Adam's apple bobbing at his throat and he came to her, pressing his palms to her cheeks. He looked into her eyes and she saw the need there. A mirror of her own.

"I want to kiss you."

She beat him to the punch, lifting herself up on her tip toes to throw her arms around his neck and his mouth was oh so gentle for about ten seconds before he opened his mouth and their tongues danced, hungry, demanding, desperate. It had been so long and she wanted this so much. Her breasts pressed to his chest suddenly wasn't enough. She wanted more of him, wanted to feel every inch of him.

But she was going to be safe even if it interrupted the mood. "Wait. I'll get a condom," she breathed. "Unless you have one, boy scout?"

He shook his head. "In my wallet. In the car. *Fuck*."

"What's your wallet doing in your car?"

"You don't live in the country, do you?"

"Come with me." Tess took his hand and led him to her bedroom, shoving him backward onto her bed. In her bedside drawer, she found her emergency stash and she tossed it to him. Connor propped himself up on his elbows, grinning.

"A box?"

"I told you things were going to get crazy."

She climbed over him, crawling up his body, tasting him

from the waistband of his trousers to his jaw. He reached for her face and they kissed as his hands tangled in her golden hair. And then she broke the kiss, panting and breathing hard against his chest, but it was only so she could inch her hands down his sides to his waist and unbuckle his belt. She tugged at the button on his trousers and then slowly unzipped him and thank fuck she had, because he was already straining, almost begging to be free. And when he was finally gloriously naked, he reached for her, pulled her down on to him and flipped her, so he was on top now, tugging at her knickers. She lifted her butt as he teased them off and then his fingers found her already slick core, Tess moaned, moving against him in a delicious rhythm as he worked and pleasured her and when she came, so fast, she bit his shoulder and cried out and his chest shook with a chuckle and he kissed the top of her head and she felt boneless.

"Holy shit," she murmured into his warm skin.

When she found her breath, and some strength, she found him, hard and ready, and guided him closer, rubbing the tip of his cock against her throbbing clit because it felt good, and then he moved and filled her and she held on for the wild ride, the bucking, the pushing against him to amp up the pressure so he could fill her up, and when he came, he shuddered and groaned and snuggled into her neck.

Holy shit again.

Tess slowly came back to earth, her breathing returning to normal.

Connor's face was still buried in her neck. He was still inside her. She gripped her thighs around him, not wanting to let go, not wanting her heart to stop thudding against her chest, wanting to savour the quivering inside her, low down, the sweet electricity of coming, the languor of her post-orgasm state.

When he lifted his head, he gazed into her eyes. Her heart rate exploded all over again.

"Tess," he whispered, and he swept her hair from her eyes. He kissed her and she melted all over again. He was a good kisser. A hungry kisser. He kissed her with every part of his body wrapped around her. She took in the slow grin on his mouth, the shadow of stubble already on his square jaw, his long nose and the lazy look in his eyes.

What did she really know about this beautiful man who'd just set off firecrackers inside her?

"Connor Hawker," she breathed deep.

He swung his legs over the side of the bed and looked back over his shoulder. If she had a bone left in her body it disintegrated into dust right there under his sexy, just-been-fucked gaze.

"Be right back."

Tess felt dizzy, drunk and high all at the same time. Her head was spinning and for the first time in a long time, her mind wasn't whirring with words unsaid or things undone. There were footsteps and then he was lying beside her again.

She turned to him, took in his handsome face. "Who the

hell are you and where did you come from?

He twisted a finger around a strand of her hair. "You have beautiful hair. It's … golden."

"Thank you. When I was a little kid, it was white-blond. I mean, all of the Harrison siblings are blonde, but I was super weird. My hair was a kind of platinum colour. You know the one that's really cool right now? No? Anyway, that's what mine was like. I always felt like a freak. And don't you think Harry, Amy and Everett pointed that out to me every chance they got? Oh, boy. I may not have been the youngest of the four of us—Everett is, by thirteen months— but they sure treated me that way. I still don't know how that happened. Maybe because I was the youngest girl or maybe because from about the age of ten Everett was already taller than me. And don't you think that drove me wild?"

There was silence next to her. Connor's eyes were soft and his expression something she didn't want to put a name to.

"You're a lot of things, but a freak isn't one of them."

"What things?" She was curious to know how he saw her, what he thought. Not that she cared, really. Maybe. Kind of.

"You're organised, smart, driven. You call a spade a spade. You've got a great career going and you have your shit together. You know what you want out of life."

She stilled. A tingling sensation shimmied up her spine and frazzled her brain for a moment.

"You know all that about me, huh? After just a week?"

He chuckled. "What else do I know? You talk a lot. You're kinda loud. You're kinda … American."

She moved quick, digging her fingers into his armpits and he jerked away from her tickling and before she knew what was going on she was on her back and he was on top of her, pinning her to the bed by her wrists.

"And you're kinda Australian, you know that?" Tess spread her legs and moved against him.

"Born and bred."

"Where exactly?"

A shadow crossed his eyes and he dropped his mouth to her left breast. When he licked her hard nipple, she squirmed underneath him and when he took it in his mouth and sucked, she pushed her hips toward him.

"You like that?" Connor licked again and looked into her eyes.

God, watching him play with her like this almost made her come on the spot. "Uh-huh," she managed and then he released one of her hands and lowered his hand, snaking it between her legs, and then he licked and teased her all over again and she bucked under his fingertips and tried not to scream.

AFTERWARD, THEY LAY side by side in bed. Tess felt sated, happy and exhausted. Was it because it had been so long between drinks for her that she couldn't remember any sex being this good? Maybe that was the benefit of a one-night stand. While you were fucking, you didn't have to think about all the things that annoy you about them, because you don't know enough about them to even have that knowledge stored in your head. How can you think about them leaving their clothes on the floor or always leaving the toilet seat up when you haven't known them long enough to know if they even do those incredibly annoying things?

Tess was beginning to realise why so many people were swiping right on their mobile phones. No-strings-attached sex was kinda fun.

"That was ..." she started, and reached across to stroke his jaw.

Connor closed his eyes and leaned into her palm.

"What happens in Vegas stays in Vegas, right?" she said.

He nodded.

"This is just sex. Right?"

"Just sex."

"Pretty incredible sex, however."

He grinned sleepily. "Yeah."

"And while we're working together, Connor, it's probably best to just pretend this didn't happen."

He paused a moment. "I can do that."

Tess didn't doubt that he would keep their secret. He seemed particularly good at keeping his own, about his life, where he was from. What he was running from.

"What's the time?" He reached over her and grabbed her phone. "Eleven. I'd better get going."

Tess spread her legs a little further and wrapped them around him. "You want to pretend this didn't happen one more time?"

He kissed her hard and fast. That was all the answer she needed. She broke the kiss, leaned in to his ear, bit his earlobe and then whispered, "Want to fuck me in the shower?"

Chapter Fourteen

TESS WASN'T SURE how she'd survived Monday.

She'd managed to avoid running into Connor most of the day. He'd been out checking on one of the new irrigation systems that was being installed in the oldest part of the property, and she'd been in the cellar with Toby, tasting from the barrels of one of Matthews' oldest cabernets, taking notes, picking his brain about the world-renowned organic processes he'd initiated so many years before.

She'd spent every hour in pent-up anticipation of another night with Connor.

An hour after he'd driven away from her place on Sunday morning, he'd had called.

"Hey, Tess."

"Hey, Connor." She'd been stretched out on her sofa, reading. Well, trying to read anyway. Nothing made sense. Her head was a fog, and bits of her still tingled from the sex. Oh my freaking God, the sex.

"Want to come over Monday night?"

She didn't need flirting or charm. She didn't need conversation about books or the weather or politics or anything.

"Yes. I do."

"Don't eat. I'm cooking."

"Okay."

"See you tomorrow. Take the stairs up the cream-and-brick building two doors down from that hairdresser's."

"Got it."

That had been it. And she'd been tingling with anticipation the whole day. And now, showered and changed, she was on her way from Wirra Station to Wirralong to meet Connor and have sex. She'd been in no doubt about the intent in his invitation or, for that matter, hers in accepting it. Two people, itches to scratch, needs to be met. Strangers in town. Sex.

She pulled into a space out front of Connor's building. It was quiet there at night. Hair Affair was closed, as was Wedding Belles, the coffee shop and the doctor's surgery. There wasn't even an all-night convenience store in this part of the world. The pub, along with any rowdy behaviour that went with such an institution, was down at the other end of the long street.

Tess blipped her electronic car lock—something Maggie still teased her about ("Who locks their car out here?")—and opened the wooden door that led to the stairwell inside. She stood at the bottom of the stairs and let herself anticipate the next few hours, maybe even the whole night. A shiver rippled through her, sending her pulse racing and her imagination soaring. She squeezed her thighs together, revelling in the delicious freedom and the sexy awareness of being naked under her flowing summer dress. She'd wanted to do something sexy for Connor and since she didn't do lingerie—too scratchy—this would do. She had a feeling he might like it.

At the top of the steps, she rapped her knuckles on the door.

Not half a second later, Connor swung the door open wide. "Hello," he said stiffly. He pulled back his shoulders and tried to block her view.

Instinctively, she tried to peer around him but he was too tall and too broad.

There was a look of panic in his eyes. "I'm sorry," he said so quietly she had to strain to hear him. "I called you. Didn't you get my message?"

Tess fished in her purse for her phone, pulled it out and saw the missed call. "It's been on silent. What's up?"

"Shit." He rubbed a hand over his hair.

From inside Connor's apartment, a woman's voice called out, "Who's at the door, Connor?"

Connor exhaled a frustration only Tess could hear. "That's my mother."

"Oh. Oh, God," Tess gasped. She was naked under her dress. She glanced down. She'd checked at home and knew it wasn't, but some irrational part of her mind had her suddenly convinced the cotton was as see-through as a pane of glass. "I'll go."

Connor's arm shot forward and he grabbed her hand.

"I'm so sorry. I don't know how long they're—"

Suddenly Connor was shoved out of the way by a petite woman with blond-grey hair in a no-nonsense style. A pair of bright red glasses were perched on her nose and she had the tan of someone who spent a lot of time outdoors. She smiled broadly. "Hi. I'm Connor's mum. Deb. Come in."

Hell in a handbasket. Tess tried to come up with an excuse not to, but the only thing that sprang to mind was to announce she'd accidently knocked on the wrong door and that she was actually looking for someone called Brad. It might have worked if she and Connor weren't still holding hands.

Connor tried to tug her in but she resisted. How the hell could they have sex *now*?

"Mum. This is Tess."

Tess's legs seemed to move of their own free will and suddenly she found herself inside Connor's apartment. She'd become untethered from Connor. "Nice to meet you, Mrs Hawker."

"It's Schmidt. I didn't change my name when I married Connor's father. But, please, call me Deb. It's so lovely to meet you, Tess. We've literally just arrived in Wirralong." Deb leaned in and gave Tess a friendly hug. "When was it, Peter? Fifteen minutes ago? And what a surprise it was! You should have seen the look on Connor's face!"

Peter stood in the small kitchen making a cup of tea at the sink next to the stove. "Hi, Tess. Nice to meet you." Tess was immediately struck by how much Connor looked like his father. They were the same height and build and she could tell by the gleam in Peter's eye and his charming smile that he would have broken hearts when he was a young man. He was maybe in his mid-sixties and seemed as fit and healthy as his wife. "We thought we might have trouble getting a park nearby for the campervan but Wirralong's not as busy as we thought." Connor's parents chuckled. Connor joined in, although his heart didn't seem to be in it.

Deb nudged her son with an elbow. "You didn't tell us about Tess, Connor."

He flashed a glance at Tess. He rubbed the top of his hair back and forth. "Tess and I work together at Matthews. She's a winemaker from California over here for a few weeks."

"Fascinating," Deb exclaimed. "We picked grapes in the Hunter Valley last year, didn't we, Peter."

"It's almost time for harvest. Were you planning on picking up some work locally? Lots of pickers descend on the district for work. Backpackers and grey nomads."

"That's us! Grey nomads. That wasn't our original plan but you've got me thinking, young lady. Maybe we should stick around for a while and work. What do you think about that, Connor?" Peter had ambled over next to his son, a question in his eyes.

"I'm sure there'll be plenty of work all around Wirralong."

"Why don't you have a seat, Tess. Connor will get dinner going." Tess gave Connor an imploring look and they had a silent conversation.

They seem really nice and all, but what about tonight?
Raincheck.
I want you.
I want you so fucking much.

Deb sat on the sofa and waited for Tess to sit next to her. The bracelets on her wrists jangled like Christmas bells. Tess noticed she had two hoop earrings in each lobe.

"So, Tess. You're an American?"

"Yes, I am. Born and bred. An all-American girl."

Peter joined them. "Fantastic place. We went to the Rockies five years ago. Incredible."

"I'm from northern California. Napa Valley. Wine country."

"We didn't get quite that far, but I hear it's beautiful. And you're working here in Australia?"

Tess explained Harrison's investment in Matthews Wines and her interest. Connor's parents seemed genuinely interested. As delicious scents began to emanate from the kitchen, Tess had almost managed to forget that she wasn't wearing any underwear, and relax into both the sofa and the conversation. It appeared Connor's parents had travelled widely. When Tess mentioned the family winery, Peter had whipped out his phone and searched for it on Google maps.

When Connor announced that dinner was five minutes

away, Deb went to set the table, Peter crossed the kitchen to fetch another beer from the fridge, and Tess excused herself to freshen up.

Connor followed her and swiftly shut the bathroom door behind him. The look on his face, a mix of horror, amusement and embarrassment, was priceless.

Tess covered her mouth to stifle the laughter that was bubbling inside her and threatening to erupt.

"I can't believe it. Their timing is …" He came to her, pulled her to him and kissed her, soft and long, and it was filled with heat and warmth and everything she thought should be in a kiss. She threw her arms around his neck and returned it, tasting him, wanting him.

She pulled back, looked up into his eyes. "Want to know a secret?"

"If it's about you, yes."

She let go of him, moved backward, reached for the hem of her dress and inch by tantalising inch, raised it.

He groaned. "Fuck. That is … that is hot, Tess. You're seriously trying to kill me right now, aren't you?"

She stifled a giggle. "And I've been sitting there all this time trying so hard not to do a Sharon Stone on your parents."

They both fell into a bout of silent laughter and then kissed each other until that particular urge had passed. Then, Connor dropped to his knees, gripped Tess's hips and pressed his lips to the curve of her hip, her stomach. His tongue darted into her belly button and she shivered. She laid her palms flat on his head and rubbed over his hair. She liked the feel of it, tiny prickles under her palm.

"I want you so much," she murmured.

Connor dropped back on to his haunches and shook his head ruefully. Tess let go of her dress and it fell like a curtain.

"Later," he said. "I promise."

"Much later, it looks like."

"They're sleeping on the sofa bed in the living room and they could be here for weeks." His eyes widened in sudden recognition. "Until the vintage is over maybe. Unless I can talk them out of it." He shot to his feet and his shoulders slumped. "Which I won't be doing. They're my parents and they're great. And they've crossed half the continent to see me."

Family. Tess understood it. Connor was lucky—more than lucky—to have both parents alive and so obviously fit and well. She couldn't get in the way of that.

"We'd better get back out there," she said. "Or they'll think we're, you know."

"When you know them better, you'll realise that's exactly what they think we're doing in here. And I wish we were, Tess."

The cogs whirred in Tess's mind. As fast as a lightning strike. As decisive as a detective in one of the crime novels she loved to read. She glanced in the mirror above the hand basin expecting to see a lightbulb burning above her head.

"You could come and stay at my place." So simple and so complicated all at once.

"What?" Connor rubbed his hair. He honestly was adorable when he was confused.

"It's a brilliant plan, even if I do say so myself. Your parents won't have to sleep on the sofa bed. They can stay here in your apartment in your bed, which I'm sure is comfortable, although I've never actually been in it, and while they're in Wirralong visiting you and picking grapes or whatever they like, you can come and stay at Wirra Station with me in the cottage. It's not big but I have a spare room. You're doing your parents a solid and I, as your co-worker, am doing you a solid. See, Connor? It's karma. Or Justin Timberlake. What goes around comes around, right? And this way, we're coworkers sharing a house. Simple."

"I can stop by whenever I like and see them, but they'll have their space and I'll have mine."

"Exactly!" Tess exclaimed.

He frowned. "My parents won't buy it. They've met you already. There's no way they're going to believe we're not sleeping together. I mean, look at you. You're gorgeous."

Tess's chest thudded. "Well, let's keep them away from Harry and Iz and Toby then. You in?"

Connor thought about. She could almost see his brain ticking over in the dark pools of his blue eyes.

"On one condition."

"What's that?"

"That I don't sleep in the spare room."

She kissed him quick. "Deal."

Chapter Fifteen

WHEN CONNOR RETURNED home from work the next day, Peter and Deb were at his small kitchen table nutting out the crossword in the newspaper. His mum was nursing a cup of tea and Peter had cracked open a beer. The sight was comforting and familiar to Connor. In the blink of an eye, he was back at home, ten years old, and it was dinner time and he'd come in from playing cricket with the kids in the street. Now, in Wirralong, a thousand kilometres from home, he could almost smell meatloaf and mashed potatoes.

"Hey, Mum. Dad."

"Hi, Connor." His mother beamed up at him. He hadn't seen them in almost a year and he could tell by the glistening expression in her eyes how much she'd missed him, which made the guilt rise in a wave at what he was going to tell them.

"We're arguing over eighteen down," Peter said.

"So what's new?" He kissed his mother on the cheek, shook hands with his father, and dropped his car keys on the kitchen bench. He stilled.

"You haven't made—"

"Your favourite. Of course I have."

"I thought I was imagining it. It smells incredible."

"My treat. I'm happy to cook while we're here, Con. As a way of repaying you for letting us stay, I mean. And I noticed the door to the bathroom is squeaking. Your father can get on to that."

"Sure can," Peter replied. "Can I get you a beer, mate? Have a seat. It's been hot out there today."

Connor sat, gladly accepted the cold beer from his father and enjoyed the cool wash down his throat.

"Mum. Dad. It's great to see you and you're welcome to stay as long as you like. But I'm going to move out and give you some space."

Talk about a conversation killer.

"But Connor, we've come all this way to see you." Their faces suddenly wore matching disappointed frowns.

"Your mother's right, mate. We don't mind about sleeping on the sofa bed. Remember all the nights we spent under the stars in our swags out near Alice Springs? When we pulled up in the old Kombi van and slept in the dirt wherever we were? Or perched up on the banks of old creek beds in the Flinders Ranges? Fun times, weren't they, Con?"

Connor smiled at the avalanche of memories they'd made as a family. "They were, Dad. For sure."

Deb had been a midwife before she'd retired and Peter had been a carpenter, but they'd never let shift work or the demands of being a tradie with his own business get in the way of their adventures with their son. Connor had had a full and happy childhood complete with labradors and the occasional guinea pig, camping trips and adventures. And all that travelling had planted the seed in him, he imagined, for the life he was living now. They'd raised him with the full awareness that the world was wide and there were always exciting things to see and do, no matter where you were and no matter how much money you had or didn't have.

And, at the heart of it, they'd shown him what a happy family looked like. A year before, when they'd hit sixty-two and Connor thirty-two, they'd officially quit work and bought their campervan so they could indulge their wanderlust and travel around Australia. They'd waited for his wedding—and instead had been there to console him—and then had taken off the week after, as planned. They would have cancelled their trip if he'd asked them to—he was as sure of that as anything—but he hadn't wanted them to stick around and watch him work through his misery. Since then, they'd travelled everywhere, picking fruit and vegetables and even flowers, from the island of Tasmania in the far south to the Northern Territory at the top end.

And now they'd landed in Wirralong to spend time with their son.

Trouble was, he wasn't ten years old anymore and the thought of sharing this small apartment with them wasn't nearly as appealing as sharing a tent when he was ten years old. How could he explain without hurting them?

"We won't get in your way, Con," Deb tried to reassure him.

Peter glanced at his wife and tried to hide his concern behind a cheery smile. "Mate, we've spent months in the campervan and believe me, the sofa bed will be way better even if it feels like one of those damn futons. Could never get comfortable on one of those no matter how hard I tried. Old bones like ours like a bit of comfort now and then and the sofa bed is a step up, let me assure you."

"Who are you calling old?" Deb jabbed Peter with her elbow, trying to suppress a smile.

"There's no way I'm letting you sleep on the sofa bed. And I'm sure you both want to use a real bathroom for a change, right?" Connor said. "Seriously. If you're going to be staying a while it's all yours. It's no trouble at all. If you want to keep cooking dinner, Mum, I'll be here every night," he teased. He was trying to butter her up, but it was true.

His parents exchanged glances and his mother released a huge sigh. "Look, we won't bullshit you, Con. We've been worried about you. That's why we're here. To check up on you, really."

"Mum ..." His rebuttal came out fast, and naturally, in the kind of tone that every son uses with his mother. But he stopped, pulled himself up. They'd seen him at his happiest and at his worst. His vow to never speak about Juliette again had meant they'd been in the dark about how he'd really been doing. It had been a protective mechanism but it had put a distance between him and his parents, which he could see now had worried them more than he'd ever thought.

He could put them out of their misery of worrying about their only child. And it could be done as simply as telling them the truth.

He put his beer down on the table. "Tess. My offer to move out... it's about Tess."

They knew him enough to wait. He had to build up to revealing himself. Tess had already picked that about him. "You're not my type," she'd said that first night they were together. "I need a man who actually likes to talk."

Deb beamed at her son's revelation. "Oh, Connor. We couldn't be happier. We know Juliette put you through the wringer. Sometimes I still feel like telling her what for, you know?"

Connor held up a hand to stop her. "Mum. I love your loyalty. But ... meeting Tess has made me realise I've actually moved on. I'm not going to look back anymore. I can't believe I'm saying this"—and the revelation was as much a shock to him as it seemed to be to his parents—"but I'm over what happened. I really am."

Was his mother tearing up? Hell, his father definitely was.

"She seems lovely. And she really knows about wine, doesn't she, Peter?"

"She does."

"She's really talented." Connor paused, rubbed his palm

over his hair. "She'll be heading back to the States soon and I want to spend as much time with her as I can before she goes. You're here and that's great. It's really great to see you. You can have the run of this place and I'll stay with Tess until she leaves or you guys do, whichever comes first."

Debbie clutched Peter's hand. Peter wiped a tear from one of his grey-stubbled cheeks.

"Settle down, you two. It's not serious. I've got to get back on the horse sometime. Dating, I mean. Well, that's what Tess calls it. Seeing women, I mean. Not that we're dating. Or anything like that."

"Well, mate. That's great. It really is. After … well, after what happened, we're so bloody thrilled to see you happy again."

Deb pushed back her chair and walked around to Connor's side of the table. She threw her arms around him in a warm embrace. "All we want is for you to be happy, Con. We'll take you up on your offer. To be honest, I've hated the bed in our campervan since we bought it. It's as stiff as a board. You go to Tess's."

"OH MY GOD. Connor."

Tess threw back her arms onto the soft pillow and blew out a breath. Connor lay next to her, his elbow propped, his head in his hand, looking at her, tracing a line down her nose, across her pillowy lips, down the arch of her neck and between her breasts. Outside, the summer wind had picked up and the bough of a gum was scraping back and forth on the tin roof, joining the whisper of the wind in an outback symphony. Being here in her bed, in her bedroom, in her cottage on Wirra Station felt somehow like camping. There was just the two of them and the wind and the trees and the stars.

"Yes, Tess?"

She giggled and grabbed for his hand, twisted her fingers in his. "I can't believe you told your parents. I thought we had a deal. Vegas and all that." She turned her head and she took his breath away. Her cheeks were flushed, her golden hair around her head in a messy halo, her lips plumped from kissing him. How had he got so lucky?

"I didn't want to bullshit them. They've been through enough."

"What do you mean? Is everything all right? They haven't come to Wirralong to tell you some bad news, or anything, have they?"

He could have sworn Tess went pale. She tried to get up, to prop herself on her elbows but he rested his hand on her chest and urged her back to the pillow. "It's all right. They're fine. They're just parents, that's all."

Telling his parents the truth had been contagious and he'd almost slipped and told Tess about his past. But he wasn't that guy anymore thanks to her, and he no longer needed to relive his failed engagement, his humiliation and regret. He didn't want her to think he was with her because he was a desperate lonely bloke who hadn't had sex in a long time. Well, the part about not having had sex in a long time had been true. Thankfully, it wasn't any longer.

"And you're forgetting that they met you yesterday. We almost fucked in the bathroom while they were right next door. I'm pretty sure they guessed without me having to say a word. So I told them."

Tess stared right into his eyes, so intensely he felt his chest thudding in response. "What did you tell them about me?"

"I said that you were an annoying motormouth American winemaker who, thank God, is going home soon."

Her eyes flared. "You did not."

"What do you think I said?"

She nibbled her bottom lip again and suddenly looked vulnerable. Was she asking deeper questions? Like, what am I to you? What do I mean to you? He wasn't ready to define what she was yet, even to himself.

"I don't know."

"I told them the truth. That I wanted to spend as much time with you as I could before you left. Okay?"

"Good answer." A smile quivered on her lips. "I like your parents. They seem super down to earth. Normal. I mean, driving around the country in a campervan? Wow. You know, it feels kind of weird that I know that they know and no one else does. I mean, I talk to people—that's what I do. I'm a motormouth, apparently. I might accidentally let something slip. What do we do then?"

Connor shrugged.

"My whole life everyone's told me I talk too much. Harry calls me Brat because when we were kids I was always getting in his face. And Amy's and Everett's." Tess smiled at a memory, her full lips curving. "'What are you doing? Can I come too? I want to play? Push me on the swing. Come for a swim.' You know—all the sibling stuff. You have any brothers or sisters, Connor?"

"No. I'm an only kid."

"Really? I can't imagine what that must have been like. And don't worry, there were plenty of times I tried. When none of them would play with me or push me on the swing or come for a swim. When my brothers were off doing their brother stuff and Amy was in her room playing with makeup, I used to lock myself in my room and wish there was only me so I had all my parents' attention." Her smile faded suddenly and she pulled her lips together. "Especially my mother's." She paused, gazing into his eyes as if she were trying to read him. "Were you ever lonely, Connor?'

"As a kid? No, never." And it was the truth. He'd only felt the sad sting and crushing ache of loneliness when he'd been an adult. When he'd hit thirty, he'd had enough of travel. He'd met Juliette and wanted to create the exact kind of family he'd had when he was a kid and, as if some kind of primal caveman instinct had risen up in him, he'd felt compelled to provide for a family, to settle, to get that dog he'd always wanted and buy a home. But he'd discovered too late that Juliette hadn't wanted any of that. How could he have been so blind to the truth?

"You will blame me for being stuck in the one place," she'd sobbed down the line to him when she'd called to cancel their wedding. He remembered how tight his tie suddenly felt around his neck, as if was being pulled taut by invisible hands, strangling him. "I cannot do it, to you or me. You made plans for us, but didn't ask me. I can't stay in Australia, have a home with you. We were crazy to think it would work between us. We are too different, Connor. We are worlds apart."

Had he been lonely as a kid? Never.

Had he been lonely as an adult? Fuck yes.

But he didn't feel that way anymore.

There was a hand on his arm. He looked down at it, at the spot where Tess's long fingers were pale against his tanned forearm.

"Are you all right, Connor? You disappeared for a minute there."

Something buzzed between them, something like an understanding, maybe more like a connection. Something way deeper than what they'd just shared.

"I was just … thinking." And he didn't know why he let her in, why he opened that little crack into his life, but it felt right, suddenly. It felt inevitable. "I was thinking about my folks. About how I'm an adult and they still worry about me. It's a pain in the ass that they do, but it's what you sign up for when you're in a family, right? And the alternative is way worse. You know, the last I heard of them they were picking blueberries in Byron Bay and then they turn up here."

"I love blueberries."

And an image came to him, of Tess with blueberry juice staining her lips purple.

"Me too."

Tess's chest rose and fell in a deep exhale. "My parents ... well, Mom died five and a half years ago, when I was twenty-three." Her voice was almost a whisper and he leaned in closer still, pressing his forehead to hers. "Dad's still running the business. I think he threw himself into it full tilt after Mom passed, like it was his way of coping. He's seventy, and semi-retired, but still can't really let go. Amy is officially the CEO now and Dad is the Chairman of the Board."

"I'm sorry about your mother."

"I still miss her. I still wish I could pick up the phone and talk to her, or sit in the big kitchen at home and watch her cooking. Everyone says I look like her, but I can't see it."

Connor swallowed something stuck in his throat. "She was beautiful, then."

Tess's eyes suddenly gleamed. "That's nice of you to say."

"It's true. And what I said about your being a mo-tormouth is also true."

Tess clapped her hands on his cheeks and pulled him in for a smacking kiss. "There's something about you, you know?" She took in every inch of his face. "I can't figure it out."

Why did he suddenly wish she'd never stop trying?

"So, back to our original problem. What am I going to tell Harry and Isabella and everyone else? This has all happened a bit quick and I haven't really had time to hatch a plan. It's all your fault. I've been too busy thinking about fucking you. And actually fucking you."

She grinned and her cheeks flushed, and Connor bent down and kissed her like it was the last time he would kiss a woman again in his whole life. He wrapped his arms around her, moved his leg over her body so he could wrap her up like a present. How was it that she still tasted like wine?

When they came up for air, Tess pinched his earlobe and continued the conversation as if nothing had interrupted her. "What am I going to say? You're living here now. I mean, staying with me. They're going to think something is going on, right? I mean, I would if I were them and someone like me was telling them that someone like you was renting a room in my house. C'mon, they're not stupid. Especially Isabella."

"What do you want to tell them?" Connor traced a finger over her breasts, and over and around her right nipple until it budded. She shot him a sizzling glance.

"What do I *want* to tell them? Let me think. I know, that I'm holding you captive in my bedroom and using you for sex."

"Works for me."

"Honestly, I'd rather they butt out of my business. But Harry's my brother and Iz is my sister-in-law. And we work together, although not for much longer. They're family. And I shouldn't keep secrets from family, should I?"

"It's your call, Tess."

"I'm not here forever. Only a couple more weeks."

"No." What was the thudding in his chest all of a sudden?

"I'll be going back to the States soon."

"Yeah."

He leaned over and ran his tongue over her nipple. Her whole body tensed and she gripped his shoulders. "Connor ..."

"Yeah?"

"Can I keep you my secret?"

"You can do whatever you like with me."

In a move worthy of a gymnast, Tess pushed him back on the bed and flipped herself on top of him. "You promise?"

Chapter Sixteen

THE NEXT SATURDAY morning at ten o'clock, Tess and Connor drove across the lawns of Wirra Station from the cottage with a car full of display tables and bottles for Matthews' first-ever wine-tasting event at Wirra Station. Tess was thankful that Connor didn't have to be at the oval to play for the Wirralong Bushrangers until one o'clock, so he had the morning free to help out.

It had been Harry's idea to ask Connor.

"You can talk about the ins and outs of the winemaking process and what you've learned about Matthews organic winemaking principles and Connor can be the muscle."

"Excuse me?" she'd gulped. Images of his shoulders and pecs and the ripples on his stomach flashed before her eyes.

"The muscle. To lift the cartons of wine. To box all the bottles we're going to sell. To load them into people's cars. You know, to help out."

And Connor would be doing exactly that. If she could keep her hands off him.

Maggie was there to greet them, waving a warm hello. "I'm so excited about today," she called out to Tess.

"So are we. This is the beginning of a long and beautiful relationship, I can tell."

Tess felt Connor by her side. "Maggie, this is Connor Hawker. I don't know if you've officially met our new irrigation manager out at Matthews."

"Nice to meet you, Maggie."

"I think I've seen you across the property," Maggie said and damn it if Tess didn't see her tongue in her cheek. "It's nice to meet you, too."

"I was actually here a couple of weekends ago for a wedding. A friend of Eddie's from Wirralong Cricket Club. Slipper and Ximena."

"Oh, that was fantastic," Maggie sighed. "He met Ximena when he was travelling in Spain and he whisked her back to Australia. The caterers did tapas and then churros for dessert. I may have tasted one or three." Maggie smiled at Tess and Tess tried to ignore the almost imperceptible lift in Maggie's eyebrows. Another silent conversation whizzed through the air. Tess stared casually into the distance.

He's hot.

Shut up.

You are, aren't you?

Can a girl be single in this town without everyone trying to hook her up?

Are you kidding? This is Wirralong, Tess.

"The vows were in English and Spanish. And Isabella learnt some phrases especially for the ceremony. Isn't she incredible? It's such a romantic story. Continents and great distances couldn't separate them. Just like Iz and Harry, don't you think, Tess?"

That was the day she'd first seen Connor, when he'd stared at her across the lawn by her cottage. When he'd caught her out wedding watching. That was definitely something she didn't want to have to explain to him.

Tess watched on as he and Maggie shook hands and made small talk. Maggie truly was an excellent actor. The Smart Ladies had been furiously exchanging messages on WhatsApp since Wednesday when they found out Connor was now officially, air quotes, "sharing" Tess's cottage. Why the hell had Tess thought she could keep Connor a secret? Tess had had to defend herself in an emergency sub-committee meeting of the club at Maggie's early on Wednesday evening.

"Sorry, Tess," Maggie had admitted. "I saw his car at your place and when it was still there in the morning, I called Isabella and asked her if anything was going on."

Tess had turned her accusing eyes on her sister-in-law. "And you put two and two together and came up with sixteen, right?"

"Hell, yes. He's hot and you're perky," Isabella had added.

"I'm not perky!" Tess had exclaimed.

"Tell us everything," Elsa had demanded congenially. "Only if you want to, of course."

Isabella had regarded her with a suspicious expression. "She's not telling. Believe me, I've tried. I've even invoked family privilege and still nothing."

"It's not complicated. Connor's parents arrived in town unexpectedly and they've been living in some kind of Winnebago while they're travelling around Australia. So, they're staying at his apartment for a few weeks and I have a spare room, so, you know. I'm just helping him out."

With his sexual tension, she'd thought. She was being a big help in that department. And he'd been returning the favour in spades.

Connor brushed by her, interrupting her licentious thoughts about him naked.

"Anyway," Tess said, trying to draw attention away from any more discussion about her secret obsession. "You said you had glasses, Maggie?"

"Here's Harry. Just in time."

"Morning all," he announced as he joined them. "Sleep well, you two?"

Tess and Connor exchanged hesitant glances.

"Me? Like a baby," Maggie replied with a wink at Tess. She swallowed the last of her coffee. "Why don't you boys set up the tables—Max is over in The Woolshed and he'll show you where the small marquee is—and Tess come with me and I'll point you in the direction of the glasses."

Connor and Harry strode off toward The Woolshed while Maggie led Tess up to the main house, through the beautifully furnished living room and to the storeroom at the rear. A four-wheeled two-tiered trolley had already been stacked with boxes of wineglasses.

Maggie leaned back against the cool stone wall and regarded Tess with a scrutinising gaze.

"So, tell me everything you didn't tell the Smart Ladies on Wednesday night."

"I don't know what you're talking about." Tess averted her eyes and fussed with opening one of the boxes to half-heartedly count and check the glasses.

"First you had a date at Janu's, which was mysteriously cancelled."

Tess gasped. "How did you know about that?"

Maggie laughed. "Small town, honey. It's half a degree of separation around here."

"Maggie, come on. I'm just helping him out."

Maggie rested a comforting arm on Tess's. "Sorry, I'm not meaning to give you the third degree. It must be all these weddings. I can't help it. I see love everywhere I look."

Tess froze at Maggie's mention of the L word. She wasn't going there, with Maggie or anyone else. There was no love between her and Connor and there never would be. The thing they had going on was about convenience and sex. And, okay sure, some laughs and a few shared dinners and wine on the verandah as the sun was setting last night.

"The thing is, Tess … you might not want to see it, but I saw the way Connor looked at you just now."

Tess looked up. She didn't want to know. "I don't know what you're talking about."

"Tess. Honey. He looks at you like Bradley Cooper looks at Lady Gaga in that movie." She sighed. "He is rather lovely. Connor, I mean. Although Bradley's not bad either. And I hear Connor's an excellent irrigation manager, too."

"He's a valuable addition to Matthews, definitely. I'm sure he and Toby and Harry will work really well together. I'm sure I'll hear all about it when I'm back in the States."

Maggie looked surprised. "I think I'd forgotten you were leaving."

"There's a lot waiting for me back home. And a future I'm really excited about."

Maggie's shoulders slumped and she crossed her arms. "Isabella was hoping … well, you know what Iz is like. I've never understood how she does it, but she has the knack of knowing in the first few minutes of meeting them if two people are going to make it. I suppose when you've officiated at as many weddings as she has, you develop a sense about these things."

"Connor and I are friends," Tess clarified. "Nothing more. I didn't come here to get involved with anyone. I don't need to complicate my time here."

Maggie smiled. "Sometimes, Tess, things get complicated when you least expect it. God, listen to me. I sound like your mother or something."

Tess swallowed the sudden lump in her throat. Tess

missed her mom so much at times like this. She knew that not all mothers and daughters were close, that not every mother and daughter shared the intimate details of their lives, but Tess had had that kind of relationship with her mother. If she could pick up the phone now and talk to her, what would she say? "Mom, I've done something crazy. I had a one-night stand with a guy who it turns out I might kind of ... *like*."

"Anyway, here are all the glasses," Maggie said. "All washed and polished thanks to my crew. Let's roll."

"WHY NOT TRY the organic riesling?" Tess poured a splash into a wineglass and passed it to a young woman on the other side of the tasting table.

"Organic? I didn't know there was such a thing."

"Matthews is one of the leading organic winemakers in Australia," Tess said, clearly impressing the woman and her friends, who'd gathered around to listen to the story. As Tess continued her conversation, Harry set out fresh wineglasses, and when the guests bought a dozen wines between them, Connor carried the carton to their car.

Tess watched him as he worked, wondering why she was still fizzing inside at the sight of him. It had only been four nights and her world seemed to have tilted on its axis. She hadn't wanted to let on to Maggie, but something had

changed in her and it wasn't just the result of four nights—
five if you counted their aborted dinner date—of exhilarating
and exhausting and oh-my-God-what-am-I-doing good fun.

Harry poked Tess in the shoulder. "Hold the fort, Tess.
I've got a meeting with a potential client over in The Woolshed. Maggie's meeting me there."

"We got this," Tess told her brother and she and Connor
watched him as he strode across the lawns looking every bit
the polished businessman.

"He's good." Connor had sidled up alongside her. She
tingled as his arm brushed her shoulder.

"He loves this stuff," Tess told him. "You've heard him.
Market share. Tariff reductions. Exports. Shipping charges.
And I'm so pleased he loves all that stuff because it means I
can concentrate on the wine. Which is the part I love. That's
why we work so well together. Why the whole Harrison
family works so well together. We're like a series of cogs in a
giant machine. We all know exactly which way to grind."

A smile quirked his lips. "A cog in a machine."

"The big wineries are like that. They need to be. We bottle half a million cases of wine each year."

"You're kidding."

"Not kidding. That's why I'm interested in organics. I
was getting a little … I don't know, lost in that big operation. I want to do something smaller. Something where I'm
closer to the process."

"And you're learning about how to do that right here at

Matthews."

Tess nodded emphatically. "In spades. When I get home, I'm going to knock the socks off my family with my plans."

"So you're going home. And you're completely okay with …" A muscle twitched in his jaw. "Our arrangement?"

Tess was taken aback. "Hold it right there, Chuck. I totally meant what I said. What happens in Vegas stays there."

Connor chuckled under his breath.

"What's so funny?" Tess propped her hands on her hips.

"Nothing."

"Tell me," she muttered. "You're doing that thing you do. You're shutting down on me."

"For one, you calling me Chuck. What is that about?"

"It's something my … we used to say in our family if someone was trying to pull the wool over someone's eyes. 'What's going on, Chuck? Who're you trying to schmooze, Chuck? What the actual fuck, Chuck?' Although that last one we said only when we were older and when we could say it without Mom or Dad hearing it."

Connor looked down at the gleaming glasses and grinned. He was finding her amusing, which she found hot.

"So, what the actual fuck, Chuck?"

His smile, so damn wide and friendly. His lips. Boy, oh, boy what he'd done with his lips. "You talk a lot, you know that?"

"So I've been told. So what if I do? I've got lots to say." She paused, undercutting her words. Just to prove him wrong. "And you, Chuck," she jabbed a finger into his hard chest. "You barely talk at all, did you know that?"

"Excuse me. What's so good about organic wine?"

Tess and Connor jolted and quickly turned eyes front, like two children caught with their hands in the cookie jar. An older gentleman wearing a peaked cap was looking over the array of bottles with narrowed eyes and a cynical expression.

"How do you do, sir?" Tess said. "I'm Tess Harrison. I'd love to talk to you about why organic wine. But first, here." Tess passed the doubting man a tasting glass. "Try it."

"Are you American?" he asked suspiciously.

"As a matter of fact I am, sir. I'm here to learn all I can from your Aussie winemakers. I'm really proud of the wine we produce back in the States too, but Matthews Wines are some of the best organics in the world."

That seemed to assuage any lingering suspicion the man had. He swirled the wine, tilted it from side to side, and stuck his nose deep into the bowl of the glass. "Not bad," he finally conceded after a few qualifying sips.

"Thank you. You see, it's not just about the taste of the wine, although that's as important for organic wine as for non-organic wine. It's about the way we produce it."

And as Tess engaged the customer with all she knew, she tried not to watch Connor out of the corner of her eye, watching her.

Chapter Seventeen

As Tess continued her almost evangelical explanation, Connor stepped back and watched. It wasn't just her passion for wine that had him looking on in awe. It was the passion she'd shared with him just hours before. He'd been at her place four nights now and each one had been filled with the sight and sound and scent of her.

He'd forgotten that fucking someone could be wild and free and fun. The last time he'd had sex, it had been loaded, weighed down with silent accusations and guilt and unspoken resentments. But with Tess, they'd shared their lust and their bodies with each other and teased and tormented each other in the way two almost strangers can, with no thought about recriminations or second thoughts.

What had started as one night was now something more, something that sat in the twilight between day and night, between meaning nothing and meaning everything. And he liked it. As he'd stepped into the shower with Tess this morning, he'd revelled in the freedom he felt to touch her, to slick her body with soap and make her come, to wash her hair, to touch every inch of her body, and in the pleasure of having every inch of his body marked by her fingertips and her lips.

He'd come to Wirralong looking for nothing but a job. Maybe that's what made it so free. There was nothing tethering them to each other but a mutual itch to scratch and a need for the touch of someone's skin, the sweet relief, the satisfaction of sex, a shared passion.

"Connor? Can you grab a box? Trevor here wants to buy a dozen riesling."

"A great choice. I'll walk it over to your vehicle, Trevor. Where are you parked?"

"Cheers, young man," Trevor said with an appreciative nod. "Not only good wine but good service too. I'll have to make the drive up from Melbourne more often."

"That's what we like to hear," Tess remarked. "Come out to the winery next time. It's gorgeous at Matthews."

"Might just do that. This way," he motioned to Connor.

When Connor returned, he slowed and took in the scene. The marquee was white in a sea of green: the carefully tended lawns and garden beds bursting with deep purple lavender and white roses, the branches of the ghost gums gently swaying overhead in the warm breeze. A gathering crowd of people were milling at the tasting table, holding glasses, talking with each other, and Tess in the middle of it all, looking cool and professional, making another sale. She swiped a credit card over her phone and then passed a bottle over to a satisfied customer, who walked away with a smile on his face, holding up the bottle of wine like a trophy as he had an excited conversation with his girlfriend.

"Hey," Tess beamed at him as he returned to her. "This is going pretty well."

He liked seeing her smile. He liked seeing her happy. Strangely, it made him feel happy too. "So I see."

"If I do say so myself, this was a good idea. The tasting."

He rounded the table and stood by her side. Closer than before. He checked around to see if anyone else was approaching. No one was. He leaned down to say quietly in her ear, because damn it he wanted to smell her perfume, "You're good at it. This."

"Yeah, I kind of am, aren't I?"

"You say you don't like the business part of the wine business, but this is it, right? Selling. You underestimate yourself."

She gave him a look of utter surprise and didn't have time to say a thing in reply as his parents had just arrived, their timing brilliant as always.

"Connor! Tess!" Deb and Peter approached the tasting table looking as if they were on their way to a hike, as they were wearing sturdy walking boots, small backpacks and wide brimmed hats.

"Hey, Mum. Hey, Dad."

"Why hello, Tess. We've come for a wine tasting. Connor mentioned you'd be here today. Isn't Wirra Station absolutely gorgeous, Peter?

"It's quite the set up," he added, gazing over the property.

"It's so nice to see you both again. Welcome to Matthews Wines," Tess said, and Connor could hear the jitter in her voice. Was his motormouth nervous? Of his parents? "Would you like a tasting? We have a riesling and a merlot."

Peter decided on the red, while Deb chose the white, and Connor looked on as they tasted, asked questions of Tess and then discussed the ins and outs of organic winemaking. He set a few more glasses on the table and twisted the caps off two more bottles. Before he knew it, his father was handing over his credit card.

"Oh, no, Peter. You don't have to pay for that." Tess waved a hand to brush him away.

"Dad, take a bottle. Really," Connor urged him. "It's one of the perks of having a son who works for a winery."

"You sure?"

"Of course we're sure," Tess smiled. "I hope you enjoy it."

Peter tucked the bottle under his arm. "Connor, any chance you could take me on a tour of The Woolshed over there? I love those old buildings. Visited lots in our travels around the place."

"Sure, Dad. You'll be all right here, Tess?" He meant the tasting but realised he'd be leaving his mother with her.

"We'll be fine, Con," Deb replied. "You two boys head off for a look around."

HONESTLY, CONNOR'S MOTHER was lovely, so why on earth was Tess so goddamn nervous?

Because she was anticipating a job interview, not a conversation. She could feel it. Wouldn't she do the same thing in her place?

"How long have you been a winemaker, Tess?"

Okay, we're starting with a general question, Tess thought. She could do that. She began to explain her family history, her studies and her travels and experience all over the world. Deb seemed fascinated.

"So I came here to Wirralong when my brother Harry married Isabella, the local marriage celebrant, and I decided to do some research."

"Is that Wedding Belles in the main street?"

"Yes, that's her."

Deb nodded. "I passed her shop this morning on my walk. I like to get up early and have a wander." She leaned in conspiratorially. "It also gives me some time on my own. Don't get me wrong. I love Peter and I love our life, but we spend a lot of time together and those campervans aren't big. Thank God neither of us snore! We would have been divorced before we started this adventure." She laughed and Tess found it infectious. "And I especially need to walk during cricket season. Honestly, if it's not the radio commentary it's the TV coverage and then the next day there's the play-by-play analysis in the newspaper and online."

Tess was shocked. "You don't like cricket?"

"God, no. Can't stand it."

"But … but … Connor loves it. He's playing for the local team, the Wirralong Bushrangers."

Deb raised her eyebrows ever so slightly and then clearly conscious of how her curiosity might appear, dropped them neatly back into place as she shrugged her shoulders. "All mothers have secrets from their sons and mine is that all those afternoons during his childhood and his teenage years when he was playing, I was secretly reading novels. I sat in my deck chair under the trees and pretended. Does that make me a horrible mother?"

Tess laughed. "Your secret is safe with me. I've seen Connor play once. Last weekend. I took a book, too, although I have to admit the whole experience wasn't as bad as I thought it would be. It was kind of relaxing sitting there listening to nothing but the wind in the trees and the birds and the occasional burst of applause. Although it takes forever, right?"

Deb considered Tess's response. "You sat through one of his cricket games?"

Tess nodded, her mind ticking over at the realisation of how that must seem to Connor's mother. "My sister-in-law Isabella tricked me into it by offering wine and a picnic. Two of my weaknesses, unfortunately. In fact, Connor's playing again this afternoon. Maybe you'd like to come along and sit with me? I have a new book to read. Jane Harper's latest."

"Oh, I've read that. It's fantastic." Deb pondered the idea for a moment. "If I go to the cricket, I'll get brownie points from both Peter and Connor. Tess, you're on."

TESS AND DEB sat in the shade of a copse of gum trees at Wirralong Oval in companionable silence reading their novels during most of the afternoon. Connor had made twenty runs before being caught out, so he was back with his team mates watching the rest of the game and his absence out in the centre made it easier for her to relax. She liked watching him play, enjoyed studying how his body moved, how he lifted the bat high and swung over his shoulder to send the red ball soaring into the trees. And now he wasn't out there, she could relax and concentrate on making a good impression on his mother.

"Another wine?" Tess reached for the bottle of wine she'd brought, the riesling, which was sitting in ice in a cooler.

"Yes, thanks Tess." Deb held out her glass and Tess filled it.

"Is Harry coming to watch the game?"

"He's had to drive to Melbourne this afternoon. Isabella works most weekends, so he tries to work around having days off when she does."

"He sounds like a very considerate man," Deb replied.

There was a loud shout from the players and Tess and Deb flicked their eyes up from their novels to see what was going on.

"He is. He's a great husband and a great brother."

"Are there just the two of you?"

"Oh, no. I'm one of four."

"Four? My goodness."

"I know, right? Mom and Dad loved kids, what can I say? There's Amy, the oldest, then Harry, then me and Everett is the youngest, although he's also the tallest, so, you know, I've always felt like the baby of the family."

"How wonderful to have a house full of children. Are there any grandchildren yet?"

"No, not yet. Amy's single, although there's nothing to stop her having a kid on her own, but she hasn't talked about wanting to do that. Harry and Isabella? Well, we're all still waiting for any news on that front. And Everett is dating his way through California as we speak. He's a real charmer. Women like him. A lot."

"And what about you? Do you want children?"

It wasn't the question that threw Tess, but the awareness of the way her answers had always been received. "No, I don't think so. At least not at the moment. Not for a few years. I just don't feel that thing that some women do about babies. And my career is really important to me."

Deb patted Tess on the hand. "And you have all the time

in the world to decide if that's the path you want to take. How old are you, Tess?"

"I'm twenty-nine in February." February 12, when she would already be home in California preparing her presentation to the board meeting, which would determine her future.

"Which date?"

"The twelfth."

Deb's jaw dropped. "What a coincidence. That's my birthday, too. Can you believe that?"

"That's incredible." Tess only became aware of the ache clenching her chest when it stole her breath. Why had talking to Connor's mother about family and children and career caused this wave of grief inside her? Because in a perfect world, she would still be able to talk these things over with her own mother. Five years gone, five years so terribly missed.

Deb patted Tess's arm. "We should have a joint birthday party, don't you think? If we're still around then, that is."

"I'll be home by then, Deb, actually."

"Oh. Right. Of course. Well, I hope you enjoy your time in Australia. Have your parents come to visit while you've been here? I'm sure they'd love to see where you're working and living, to meet your friends."

Tess's pulse hammered. She splayed a hand to her chest to stop her heart exploding out of it. "Amy and Everett and my Dad came over for Harry and Isabella's wedding. They had such a great time. They petted a koala and even climbed the Harbour Bridge while they were in Sydney. But Mom ..." A deep breath, then another. "Mom died a few years ago."

There was a moment of heavy silence between them. "Oh, love. I'm so sorry to hear that. I know I've just met you, but you seem like a good egg to me. And Connor thinks so much of you and that's recommendation enough. I'm sure your mother would have been so proud of you with all you've accomplished, with the person you've become." Deb reached for Tess's hand and Tess took it. She held on, squeezing her eyes closed, trying to imagine it was her mother's tanned hand in hers, trying to hear her mother's voice instead of Deb's. But she couldn't summon the sound of it, or the feel of her hand. There was already a new voice in her head.

You have all the time in the world to decide if that's the path you want to take.

It was pretty good advice. It was motherly advice. They were words of wisdom from someone older and wiser, who didn't know her. So why did it feel as if it had been tailored just for her? She squeezed Deb's hand in return and they let go. Their books sat closed on their laps.

"Tell me about Connor as a kid," Tess said. "What was he like?"

Deb's expression was one of joy and pride. "He was a lovely boy. And not much has changed, I don't think, but I

am biased. He didn't love school so much, but loved working with his dad in the big shed we had in our backyard,
making things, repairing things. He was always cheery. There
were only the three of us, you see. We were a pretty tight-
knit little group."

"You didn't have any other children?"

A sad smile. "I would have loved to have had more, but it
didn't work out."

"I'm sorry to hear that."

Deb sat back in her chair and looked over to the
clubrooms, where Tess could see Connor sitting, watching
the play. "It took us a long time to have Connor. I had
polycystic ovary syndrome and it was hard to get pregnant
again. There was always the option of IVF back then, and
Peter and I thought very seriously about it for a while, but in
my line of work I'd seen too many women who had pinned
their hopes on it and were so sadly and cruelly disappointed.
So in the end we put that dream away and considered
ourselves so lucky to have Connor. That's not to say it wasn't
hard, though. Imagine it. Me, a midwife and being around
all those babies and those new mums. I'll confess, sometimes
I held it all in and barely got home before the tears started."

Tess wasn't angry anymore about losing her mother. It
was more a constant, nagging ache for all that she had missed
out on with her. Every time something good happened, she
couldn't help but feel that way all over again.

Deb rested her book in her lap. "In the end, I decided it

was no use railing against all the unfairness in the world. It only makes a person bitter. I'm sorry, Tess. I don't know why I'm telling you this. It's just that I've been surrounded by men in my house—even our dogs were boys—and it's nice to talk to another woman for a change."

Tess held her glass to Deb and they clinked. "I'm all ears."

"And you're all heart. I can see that. I'm glad Connor found you."

"Oh, we're not …" We're not what, Tess thought. Dating? Serious? What had started out as no-strings-attached sex had changed into something else. Something she might actually miss when she went home.

"Whatever you are, you're doing him the world of good. After the disaster that was his wedding day, we thought he'd never meet someone else. He was so devastated, the poor thing, understandably."

Tess froze. Deb must have noticed her shock because a hand slowly rose to her mouth and covered it as if she were trying to push the words back in. "Oh no. He hasn't told you."

All Tess heard was wedding day. Wedding day. Wedding day. The words ran round and round in her head on an interminable loop.

"Connor's married?" Tess asked slowly, trying to take it in.

Deb's face fell. "I may as well tell you now. Connor was

engaged, Tess. His French fiancée left him standing at the altar. She simply didn't turn up. That's why we're here. To check up on him. You see, we're not sure he's got over it."

Chapter Eighteen

TESS HELD THAT information about Connor's engagement and abandonment close to her chest for the rest of the afternoon. She assured Deb that she would keep secret the inadvertent revelation and managed to carry it off all evening, throughout a chatty dinner with Connor and his parents at the pub in Wirralong, and on their drive back to Wirra Station.

The first thing she did was jump in the shower so the running water would disguise the sound of her sobbing. How could she have been so stupid? She'd let a one-night stand turn into something more in her head, had started to feel something for Connor, something deep and real. He'd always been secretive about his past and know she knew why. He was still in love with something else. She let the water run over her tense shoulders and through her hair to try and get rid of her headache, until she was all cried out. Then she dressed, ran a towel through her hair, and opened her laptop to look for the cheapest flight back to the States. It wouldn't be long now, just a couple of weeks to the all-important Harrison family board meeting, which had been scheduled during a quiet time in the northern hemisphere wine industry.

The grape picking was about to begin—Harry and Toby had organised casual pickers through an agency in Wirralong, and they were about to descend on Matthews and other wineries in the region to harvest the grapes. The place would become a hive of activity for weeks and weeks, with caravan parks filled to capacity, temporary accommodation on properties filled with backpackers looking to earn some money to finance the rest of their travels, and Connor's parents. Peter and Deb had secured themselves jobs at Matthews, courtesy of Harry's happy intervention.

The grapes were already deep in veraison; the red grapes were ripening and had almost completely turned from green to dark and their increasing sweetness meant picking would begin soon. The crop size seemed healthy and if the hot weather continued the way it had been in northern Victoria, the ripening would accelerate. It was a sight that Tess never tired of, as it was always filled with so much promise. The vines filled with grapes the colour of those green varieties you might see in a fruit bowl in someone's kitchen, now blushing a light pink and then transforming to a deep purple, with a shimmer of white clouding the colour.

It killed her to be leaving before vintage, but she had no choice. Her board presentation needed to be prepared and she couldn't do that in Wirralong with Connor so close. Because being with him was addictive and the thought of

TESS

being without him had suddenly become an ache deep inside her, gnawing at her independence, her plans and her future. She and Connor had made no promises to each other so why did this feel like a heartbreak when she'd never given her heart to him in the first place?

She needed to leave.

Footsteps. Connor had padded in his bare feet to her side.

"Tess? What are you doing?" He yawned. He sounded sleepy. She was tired, too. They hadn't been getting much sleep, with all the sex and all the midnight conversations they'd had. Conversations in which he'd clearly held things back from her.

She lifted her chin. "I'm booking my flight home."

She didn't have to look up to feel the tension coiling in him. It was as if something snapped in the air between them.

"Already?" He rubbed his hair. It no longer stood up now, but was softer, blonder.

Tess didn't raise her eyes from her laptop screen. She couldn't. "I think I can get a flight next week. Fingers crossed."

Connor dropped his butt on the coffee table opposite her. Their knees knocked as he sat and her laptop almost took a tumble to the floor. They both reached for it, their knuckles clashing.

"Shit, sorry."

"No, I'm sorry." They both spoke at the same time and

167

looked up into each other's eyes.

"You're leaving."

Tess nodded. "This shouldn't be a surprise to you, Connor."

And it shouldn't be hurting her so much, either. But knowing that he'd been engaged, that he'd been looking for that happy ever after had rocked her. She'd wanted no-strings-attached sex and she'd clearly picked the wrong guy for that. Connor was the kind of guy who wanted forever, who wanted a future. She couldn't offer that to him. And it was best that whatever it was they had ended now before ... hell, before she didn't want to go.

What had happened to her? Four weeks in Australia and she was beginning to doubt herself. She closed her eyes, breathed deep, tried to remember that conversation with her mother when she'd been fifteen years old.

Getting married and settling down with a family changed all that for me.

But why, Mom?

Because that's the way it was then. But it doesn't have to be that way for you. I want you to dream big, Tess.

Getting married and settling down had changed everything.

Tess remembered her vow, her promise to her mother to never give up on her big dreams. And her determination to do what her mother was unable to was still as strong as ever in her heart.

Not even stumbling across a perfect guy like Connor Hawker would distract her from that ambition.

Because he seemed like a perfect guy.

And she loved him, which was totally freaking inconvenient.

And what was she about to do to the perfect guy she loved? Leave him just like his fiancée had.

"I guess it's snuck up on me a bit faster than I thought," he said, his voice flat. Still, the sound of it seeped inside her, warmed her, worried her.

"It's been fun, Connor, but it's time for me to get back to my world and to leave you in yours." Her fingers hovered over the keys. She wanted so desperately to search for *ways to mend a broken heart.*

"Fun? Yeah. It has been fun." He looked tired and confused and as if he'd opened a novel halfway through and was trying to pick up the threads of the plot.

She clicked the keys. "Awesome. I think I might have found a seat for next Sunday. Isabella will no doubt be working, so I'll ask Harry to drive me to Melbourne."

Connor reached over and slowly pushed down the lid of the laptop until it clicked closed. "Wait just a minute."

Tess opened it.

"Please, Tess. You don't have to keep up the act. My mum called me just now when you were in the shower. She told me that you know about what happened on my wedding day."

Her heart began to pound. "I'm sorry for what happened to you. It must have been awful."

"It's freaked you out, hasn't it?"

"No. It's none of my business, really. It's fine."

Connor rubbed his eyes and took a deep breath, as if he were steeling himself for something. "Listen, please, Tess. I didn't tell you because ... how can I explain it? Since I met you, I haven't felt like that guy anymore. And I haven't wanted to be that guy for a really long time. For the first time in a year, since I was humiliated in front of my family and all my friends and everyone I worked with and, I mean, we'd really gone all out and invited everyone we knew and the local butcher, because I was so damn happy about marrying her." He shook his head ruefully at the painful memory. "For the first time in a long time, I don't feel like a fuckwit. I feel like a regular guy again. A pretty lucky guy, actually."

Tess didn't want to read the meaning in his expression.

"And that's felt fucking great. I didn't want that bit of my life to bleed into this bit. The really good bit. Right now, you're about the best thing that's ever happened to me. I didn't want to think about the past at all, much less dredge it all up again. I had to stand up in front of everyone and announce that Juliette wasn't coming. Imagine what that was like?" His tone was accepting, not angry or resentful, although from where Tess stood he had every right to be both. With bells on.

"I can't," Tess whispered, almost dumbstruck. That was perhaps the longest speech Connor had ever made. Mr strong-silent type was maybe not so silent after all when it came to matters of the heart. She blinked back the tears and willed herself to hold her tongue and simply listen.

"I've moved all over the country trying to forget about her. And nothing worked until I came to Wirralong and found you. You're like a ray of sunshine, you know that? Like … the first shoots on a grapevine, you know that stage in spring when they're Granny Smith apple-green and about to burst to life and you just know that if nothing eats them or they don't get downy mildew, they're going to flourish and grow into something beautiful before you can blink."

Oh no no no no no. That was perfect.

"I know your heart was broken, Connor. Mine would have been, too, after what she did to you. But this? You and me? It's not what you think it is. I'm just the next woman who came along. It could have been anybody, but it just happened to be me. And that's okay, really. No hard feelings. I was always going to go home to make my life and career there. You're a wonderful guy and it's been fun."

Keep talking and you'll convince yourself. Keep talking and don't look at him.

"Fun? You're so much more to me than that, Tess."

Her head buzzed like a thousand bees had created a hive inside her head. Her vision blurred. "I have a plan for my life, Connor. I'm not going to change that for anyone."

"Who says I'm asking you to change anything?" There was a note of frustration creeping into his voice.

"You haven't yet, but you will. And I'm not going to change for anyone, got that? I'm going home to make sure my dreams come true and nothing is going to stop me, Connor. Not even no-strings-attached sex with a hot Australian guy."

Not even if I love you.

He stood and paced the room. "Hang on, I get it. Now that you know about my past, you think I've got too much baggage for you. Well, look around, Tess. That perfect guy you're after doesn't exist. You're waiting for a prince to come, and that only happens in the movies. Snow White, right?"

Oh, how she wished she could control her tears, but they flowed. And the rest of her story tumbled out. "That was my favourite movie when I was a child. It was my mom's favourite, too. We used to watch it, just the two of us, sprawled out on the living room floor in our big house. We always had popcorn. And Mom would sing that song to me every night to get me to sleep. About my prince coming and what a thrill that moment would be. But I put away that dream of finding a prince because you know what? Those princesses don't get to live their dream and start their own wine label, do they? No, they end up stuck in some castle after they get married, wearing ridiculous poufy dresses, settling down and raising four kids."

Tess felt dizzy. Those bees were back. Why had she never realised it before? That was her mom. The princess in the castle who'd given everything up for her prince.

She lost all her breath in a giant exhale and suddenly felt weak.

"You want to start your own label? You never told me that."

"Well, I do. I don't want to be a cog in the gigantic Harrison Wines machine. That's why I'm here. To learn all I can before I put my proposal to the board."

Connor stood, paced to the window and stared out at the view. From behind, the tension in his shoulders was evident as he crossed his arms.

"You're waiting for a prince." He turned, shattered. "There's no way I can compete with that, Tess."

He walked past her toward the bedroom. A few minutes later, he walked back out through the living room, fully dressed, his overnight bag in his hand. "Here's the spare key." He put it gently on the coffee table in front of her. He went to the door, reached for the handle and stopped. He didn't look back when he spoke.

"Good luck with the label. You'll be great at it."

And by the time Tess wiped her tears away, he was gone.

Chapter Nineteen

WHEN CONNOR BLINKED his eyes open the next morning, exhausted from a night of fitful sleep on the too-short sofa in his apartment in Wirralong, two very concerned faces peered down at him.

He startled. "Mum. Dad. You scared the shit out of me. How long have you been watching me sleep?" Connor sat up slowly, his eyes adjusting to the light. He'd kicked off his shoes when he crept in late the night before, but was otherwise still fully dressed. It had been a long and lonely drive back to Wirralong from Wirra Station, Tess's words swirling round and round in his head.

It's been fun, Connor, but it's time for me to get back to my world and to leave you in yours.

"You all right, Connor?" Deb asked, assessing his rumpled clothing. She looked around. "Where's Tess?"

He briskly rubbed his hair. "She's at home. At her place, I mean."

Deb and Peter glanced at each other. "And you're here?" Peter asked.

Connor believed that question didn't need any further

clarification from him, so he didn't answer it.

"Would you like something to eat? I can make you scrambled eggs or a bowl of something," Deb offered. There was a touch of panic in her voice.

"No, thanks. I don't think I'm hungry."

Connor closed his eyes to obliterate his overwhelming sense of deja vu. Had he woken up and been whisked back in time? His parents were peering into his face, wondering if he was going to fall apart. He'd just been dumped by a woman he loved. The only thing missing was the disappointed crowd of family and friends and the pitying stares.

Yeah, he loved her.

He'd stupidly fallen for Tess, hadn't he, like the biggest glutton for punishment in the world. Maybe he had a predilection for being dumped by women with foreign accents. Maybe that's why he couldn't seem to find an Australian woman to fall in love with, one who was perfectly content to stay here with him and make a life together under the gum trees and the Southern Cross.

He slowly stood and tensed as his back spasmed. He needed a paracetamol. And a stiff drink.

"Before you ask, it's over with Tess and me. I'm not going into any other details because they're private. But it's done. She's going back to the States. And fuck it, I'm going to get myself a dog. Excuse my language. I want one of those dogs that looks at you like you're a plate of dog food. Like a nice big bone. A golden retriever. A red heeler, maybe."

Connor ambled to the kitchen and put the kettle on the stove. Peter and Deb shuffled after him, hovering.

"A dog would be good," Peter said. "Heelers need a lot of exercise and love the big open spaces. That'd be the perfect dog to take out in the vineyard with you."

"Exactly," Connor agreed.

"The thing is, Connor. We know you're a grown man and you don't need our advice," Peter said.

Connor filled a glass from the tap and lifted it to his lips. "But you're going to tell me anyway, right?"

"Come sit down, love." Deb moved to the table. Her husband followed. He knew they were building up to something important. They'd never been the kind of parents who were perpetually disappointed in his life decisions. In fact, from the earliest age they'd supported him in everything he'd ever done. He'd always got the message loud and clear that they only ever wanted him to be happy. He loved them for that, always had and always would.

"There's something we need to be honest with you about."

"Yeah, Mum. What is it?"

"We've been holding this in a long, long time. The thing is, and this is hard to say even now after all this time—"

Peter ploughed on in. "But it's easier now because you didn't marry her ..."

Deb nodded in emphatic agreement.

Connor's shoulders stiffened. "You're talking about Juliette?"

"Yes, love. The thing is, we never really liked her. She was tremendously snobby and she treated me like I'm a complete bogan. I tried really hard to have a decent conversation with her, time and time again, to get to know her a little, but she just wasn't interested in getting to know me."

Peter harrumphed. "We just never had a good feeling about her, Connor."

"And there I was, having only just met Tess and we had a deep and meaningful conversation at the cricket that was more open and honest than I ever had with Juliette in all the time you were together. And we never said anything because you chose her and it's your life."

Connor reeled. "And you're telling me this because?"

"We're glad she dumped you. There. I've said it. It's hard, but there it is. And we came to Wirralong to see you and to make sure you'd got over that Frenchie, that's what." Peter made a fist and gently bumped it on the kitchen table. That was about as hardcore as Connor's father got. He was a sweet and gentle man who wouldn't hurt a fly, which made the fact that he was saying this to Connor kind of huge. And entirely unnecessary, as it turned out.

Where should Connor start? "You both think I'm still in love with Juliette?"

"Well, isn't that why you and Tess broke up?"

"Shit, no."

"Then why, son?"

"Because …" Connor tried to figure out what had happened the night before, and ten hours later he still couldn't quite figure it out. Had Tess dumped him because he wasn't perfect? And then it came to him, clear as a bell.

"Fuck. She dumped me because she knows I've fallen in love with her."

"Have you?"

"Abso-fucking-lutely. Yes. I have."

Peter banged his fist on the table with all the strength he could muster. "That's bloody marvellous, Con."

Connor shrugged. "Not so bloody marvellous as it turns out, Dad. She's going home and it turns out she's not in love with me."

"Are you completely sure about that?" Deb asked.

"She told me herself last night. She said what we had was only a casual thing, a bit of fun." And as the words floated in the air, Connor rewound the scene from the night before. He really was a stupid fuckwit. He hadn't told her. He could've tried to convince her that he could be her prince, the kind who didn't want to get in the way of her dreams. She deserved a happy ever after and so did he, their way. He gathered his parents together in a tight group hug. "Good talk. I've gotta go."

"Go get her, Connor," Deb cried.

"You're back on the horse, Con," Peter announced. "Go get her."

Chapter Twenty

"CHOP IT ALL off, Elsa."

Tess stared at herself in one of the mirrors lining the walls at Hair Affair and watched Elsa's calm reaction. It was the exact opposite of hers. Her wide eyes and her pinched lips were betraying her. She was still in shock from the realisation that Connor loved her and that she loved him.

It was a long moment before Elsa responded. "Are you sure?"

Tess lifted her chin and stared herself down. "Absolutely."

"Look, Tess. It's Sunday. In about an hour, this place is going to be heaving with brides and mothers of the bride and matrons of honour and bridesmaids and flower girls." Elsa rolled her stool around to Tess's side and her eyes drifted from Tess's locks to her face. Her expression one of calm kindness. "This is your decision. Absolutely. But I've done this job a while and I get to know things about people. When someone comes in here asking me to chop of all their hair, two things are up. Either they've just broken up with someone and they want to make a big life change. Or two, they are too shit-scared to make the big life change they're considering so they go with the hair, which is something they always come to regret later. It always baffles me that people think hair is easier. It can take years to grow back, you know."

Even Tess could see how wide her own eyes had flared and how her mouth had fallen open. She knew Elsa did good hair, but now she was a psychic as well?

"So, which is it, Tess? Heartbroken or shit-scared?"

For once, possibly only the second time in her life, Tess found herself lost for words. Was it possible to be a little bit of both—heartbroken and scared? "It's …" Tess watched her eyes fill with tears and decided she was truly pathetic. "Connor. I don't know what to do."

Elsa slipped her comb and scissors onto the tray on wheels by her side and sighed. "Honey, you don't need a haircut. You need an emergency meeting of the Smart Ladies Supper Club. You stay right there. I'll see who's on call."

TWENTY MINUTES LATER, Tess was still in the chair, wearing her gown and a haunted expression. Elsa, Isabella, Serenity, Maggie and Lady Emmaline were staring at her as if they were a jury deciding her fate, having just heard some rather unsettling new evidence.

"I call this emergency meeting of the Smart Ladies Supper Club to order. Does anyone mind if I start off the round table discussion?" Maggie asked, biting into a Tim Tam. "By the way, thanks for bringing the supplies, Iz," she said.

"They're absolutely mandatory when making major life decisions. Or for watching rom-coms."

"They'd better help." Tess leaned forward and took a huge bite of the chocolate coated biscuit in her hand. "This is one Australian tradition I'm willing to embrace, Isabella. Ladies, I need your advice. I'm kind of stuck between a rock and a hard place."

"You've come to the right place and the right group of women," Emmaline said with a nod of her graceful head. Her hair didn't even move when she did. "Perhaps we can provide some independent counsel, having no vested interest, other than we all like you very much.

"That's very kind of you to say," Tess said. "But I—"

Isabella held her index finger to her lips. "Tess. Settle. This is the bit where we ask you some pertinent questions. That'll help us advise you in the most appropriate way."

Tess couldn't make this decision on her own. I'm not your mother, Maggie had told her. But I need one right now, Tess thought. What would mom tell me to do?

"So," Serenity said. "You and Connor."

Tess nodded. "Me and Connor."

Emmaline pondered. "Is it serious?"

Tess bit her lip and started bunching up the black gown in her hands. "It wasn't at first. It was a what-happens-in-

Vegas-stays-in-Vegas kind of situation."

Isabella groaned and held her head in her hands. "God, Tess. Nothing *ever* stays in Vegas. Aren't Harry and I proof of that?"

"We were going to keep it casual. No strings attached, because I'm going home. And it was, until it wasn't. First, I thought he was fun. And then that turned into like, and then deep like and now … I'm pretty sure he could be the one. The perfect one."

"Oh, how marvellous to find the one," Emmaline sighed.

"It's not marvellous at all, Lady Emmaline," Tess said.

"Why not?" Isabella demanded.

"Connor and I broke up."

All four women stared at Tess.

"What happened?" Isabella whispered.

Tess looked at each of their faces. "There's something I need to tell you about Connor."

Elsa smirked. "I hope he's not on the run from the cops or something. Although that could explain the whole strong silent type thing he's got going on."

"The cops? No, nothing like that. He's kind of on the run from … well …"

Now she had everyone's attention. You could have heard a pin drop in the salon.

"A broken heart. A year ago he was jilted at the altar. His wife—I mean fiancée—hang on, ex-fiancée—hopped on a plane back to Paris the day of their wedding. She called him and he had to tell his family and all their guests that the wedding was off."

Maggie frowned. "Poor Connor. How could anyone do that? It's cruel, don't you think?"

"Crueller than going through the whole thing and then having to get a divorce?" Elsa asked.

"The thing is, I didn't know. If I'd known, I wouldn't have got involved with him, because he's clearly on the rebound and not a safe bet because his heart still belongs to someone else."

"I don't think it does," Isabella said. "I think his heart belongs to you, dear Tess."

"It can't. And mine can't belong to him, either."

"But it does already. Am I right?" Maggie's face was a picture of kind understanding.

"I've really fucked this up. The thing is … he's not supposed to be the one. He's not right for me in any way. He's not The Perfect Guy."

Emmaline exchanged glances with Maggie and Isabella. "You two have met him. What's wrong with him?"

"Nothing that I've noticed," Isabella said.

"He seems lovely."

Tess felt her chest puff up. She'd gone over the reasons why and she felt comfortable in this territory. "He barely talks at all."

Isabella rolled her eyes. "Imagine if you met someone who talked as much as you do? No offence, Tess, but neither of you would ever get a word in edgewise. You're a chatty Cathy. He's the strong silent type. It's yin and yang. You're a good match."

Emmaline, Maggie, Serenity and Elsa nodded in agreement.

"Wait, there's more. His hair is too short. He doesn't care about personal grooming."

"You want a show pony?" Serenity looked taken aback.

Maggie chimed in. "And don't you walk around in steel-capped boots most of the time?"

"And," Elsa added, "weren't you just half an hour ago asking me to cut off all your hair?"

"And ... and he doesn't seem to want to settle down in one place."

"Neither do you, Tess," all four women chorused.

"He's Australian and I'm American."

"Your brother made it work with Isabella," Maggie told her. "That's not a reason if you really love him, Tess."

"That's right, he did. And let me clarify," Isabella said. "Your brother's not perfect, Tess. And for that matter, neither am I, not by a long shot. But you know what? I love him because of that, not in spite of it. When you really love someone, you love them for everything they are, warts and all. For all their imperfections."

Tess felt lightheaded all of a sudden. She pushed herself forward on her stool and ripped off her black gown. "I've got to go find Connor before it's too late."

Chapter Twenty-One

E LSA SCRAMBLED FOR her keys and hurriedly unlocked the front door of her salon. The Smart Ladies all but shoved Tess out into the street. The first thing she saw was his vehicle, parked right there on the street behind his parents' campervan and her heart leapt to life inside her chest, giving her a power surge of courage. The last thing she heard as she took off was Isabella calling out after her, "Go, girl!"

She stopped and looked back, suddenly all too aware that what she was about to do was going to change her life. At least she hoped her life would change. If Connor could forgive her. If she wasn't too late. Her heart galloped and she pressed a hand over her heart. She could do this. She could be brave. She could take the risk of winning him back. And in that moment, she knew she would be okay, whatever happened, because she'd survived heartbreak far worse than a rejection. She looked up to the morning sky, wisps of cloud streaked across it like an angel's shimmering gown.

"Wish me luck, Mom," she whispered and squeezed her eyes closed for a moment.

Then, twenty quick steps to Connor's. She pressed her palms flat on the wooden door leading off the street and pushed with all her strength before racing up the flight of stairs to his front door. She didn't even wait a moment to recover her breath before she made a fist and pounded. "Connor. It's me. Please God be here." She pounded some more. "Ow, that really hurts." She sucked on her knuckles, suddenly red from her knocking. "Connor, I know you're there. Your car's parked out front. Please open the door. We need to talk. Or, at least I need to talk and you need to listen, which is kind of our default position. Please, Connor."

She waited. Pressed her ear to the door to listen out for any sounds from inside. Were there footsteps? She almost flattened her ear trying to decipher what it was. A possum in the roof maybe?

"Connor!" She knocked and knocked and vowed not to stop until he opened the door. One. Two. Three. Four. Five.

"Connor. It's me. Open up. Please."

Six. Seven. The door swung open.

"Connor." A shot of almost uncontrollable relief, quickly followed by lust, surged through her like adrenalin. She stifled the urge to throw her arms around him and never let go, because she would have crushed the huge bunch of flowers he held in one hand. "Tess." He looked blindsided.

"Where are you going?" she asked, breathless from all the shouting.

"To find you," he replied, holding up his car keys, which

jingled in the space between them. "What are you doing here?"

"I need to talk to you." She moved quickly past him into the living room. There was so much she needed to say. "Can we sit?" She gestured to the leather sofa. "I'd definitely feel better if we were sitting. There are things I need to say and …" She sucked in a deep breath. "My legs feel kind of wobbly and I need to sit down." Tess didn't wait for a reply. She walked over and sat, primly, her hands on her knees like a schoolteacher in an old movie. And then shot to her feet.

Connor watched her, a wry smile on his face. "Okay, so you're not sitting."

She cocked her head at the flowers. "Are they for me?"

He walked over and gave them to her. "Yes."

"They're lovely. That's very nice of you. There's something I need to say to you, Connor. The thing is. The thing …" Tess's thoughts tumbled inside her head, like clothes in a spin dryer. Sentences crashed into words and thoughts tangled with all she'd been planning to say until it all disappeared in a huge muddle.

There were noises from the kitchen and Connor chuckled. "Mum, Dad. You can come out."

His parents slowly emerged from the kitchen, looking sheepish. "Hi, love," Deb said.

"Hi, Peter. Hi, Deb. Nice to see you again."

"We'll just go for a walk, shall we, Deb?" Peter tried to surreptitiously usher his wife toward the door. "Let you kids have some privacy."

"No, really. I'd like you to stay," Tess said, surprising herself.

Connor gazed at her. "You would?"

"I want your parents to hear what I have to say."

She lifted her eyes to the ceiling. *Mom, I'm here. I almost blew it but I have a second chance. Help me. Give me a sign, will you? How should I tell him?*

There was silence except for the sound of her breathing. There was no bolt of lightning or flash of inspiration. It was all up to her now.

She gently laid the flowers on the dining table and went to Connor.

Could he hear her heart beating from this distance? "The thing is, Connor. I'm not perfect." She closed her eyes. Waited for her thoughts to settle, her heart to stop racing, for the next sentence to form in her head. "Maybe it's about time I gave up on the idea of perfect and embrace messy and imperfect. And that's scary. Because messy is real."

She waited.

He didn't say a word but the look on his face: oh, it was everything. He was looking right at her, his pupils wide and open. His gaze dropped to her mouth and his Adam's apple bobbed up and down as he swallowed.

From across the room, Deb's breath hitched and Peter cleared his throat.

"My mom was fierce for me. She wanted me to have all

the things she didn't. You know, she was a winemaker before she married my dad and she gave it all away when they married and had kids? Or, most likely, she was forced to give it all away. She always encouraged my dreams. 'Dream big,' she used to say to me. And I've kept that thought close all these years, that I was building my career not just for myself, but for my mom, too. I was doing what she wasn't able to. And every guy I've ever met has wanted to change me, to turn me into their perfect woman. And I wasn't going to change myself to fit someone else's idea of who I should be. But just now I remembered something else she said to me, when she was in hospital. Her last words to me before she died were 'Be happy.' And all these years I thought that my ambitions for my career would be the things that would make me happy. So if I was going to let any man into my life, he'd have to be crazy perfect and that was convenient because no one could ever measure up to that insane stand-ard. Every man I've ever met has tried to change me. Until you."

Connor, Peter and Deb watched her.

"Sweetheart, that's—"

"Wait, Mum," Connor interrupted. "There's more."

Tess reached for Connor's hands and held them tight. "My mom was a fairy princess. I'm not. You know me." And her breath hitched at the words she'd just spoken. He did know her. "I'm *so* not. I mean, I wear steel-capped boots to work. I'm just not built for that big fairy tale happy ever after. But she would have given that to me. She would have given me the perfect wedding, you know? The rose-covered arbour. The perfect dress, just the right shade of ivory. She would have picked the perfect flowers and the right food and even the music. Definitely no techno. Because she knew me and she knew what would be perfect for me. She was that kind of mom, you see? And I've pushed you away with excuses about our Vegas deal, about having to go home, because the thought of her not being there for my wedding ..." Tess didn't realise she was crying until her tears cooled on her cheeks. "And not that we're even close to thinking about that, especially you after what happened, but you see, I think you're the one. I think if I ever did want to get married, it would be to you. And that scares the hell out of me."

Connor lifted her hands to his lips and kissed her knuckles one by one.

"And then I met your mom and that made it harder instead of easier. Because she's so lovely. And your Dad, too." Tess sniffed. "And that made me miss my mom so much more. So there it is. You weren't just some fling, Connor. From the beginning, you were always so much more."

"You finished?" He took her in his arms and lowered his forehead to rest on hers.

"Almost. But there's one more thing I need to say." Tess took a deep breath. "I love you, Connor Hawker."

His blue eyes sparkled in the clear Wirralong light pouring through the tall windows. "That's good. Because I'm in love with you, Tess. And I will follow you anywhere, any place, if you'll have me. Here, California, Timbuktu. Anywhere with a vineyard. I was coming to find you to tell you that. I'll do whatever it takes to be with you and to help you make your dreams come true. All of them. Me and your own label. We can do it together."

And when Connor held her tight, the drumming of his heart, that enormous heart, was evidence enough that what he'd said was true. "Nothing about love is perfect, Tess. It's imperfect. It's messy and it will drive you nuts sometimes. And I'm no prince."

Tess laughed with relief and joy. "You're perfect for me, and that's all that matters."

And when they turned to Connor's parents, they joined them in shedding happy tears.

"Welcome to the family, love," Deb sniffed as she clapped her hands together in delight.

"Connor, mate," Peter added proudly. "I've got a real good feeling about this one."

Epilogue

Two years later…

"CONNOR," TESS CALLED. "Hurry up! The number's ringing! They'll pick up any minute!"

From across the kitchen in their home on the sprawling grounds of the Harrison family estate in Napa Valley, California, Connor padded over the polished floorboards holding two glasses of wine. They'd just finished dinner—Connor had quickly whipped up a delicious pasta dish and Tess had rinsed the dishes and stacked the dishwasher—and were now waiting for the FaceTime call from Wirralong.

It was a cold January and a fire was roaring in the fireplace in front of them. They'd had a busy day out in the vineyards, which would provide the grapes for their new label, Motormouth Wines. The vines had been pruned and were still bare, and Tess was counting down the days until spring and the first show of new life on the project she'd worked so hard to get up and running. Motormouth wines were going to be completely organic, environmentally sound and absolutely delicious. The vineyard would run on biodynamic principles and would recycle as much waste as it could. It was her dream and Connor was helping make it come true.

She looked down at the knotted rug in front of the stone fireplace on which their one-year-old chocolate labrador, Chuck, was fast asleep. The Chuckster had spent all day outside with his master as Connor had been installing a line of drip irrigation in the fiano vineyard, and the pup was exhausted.

"Here's your champagne, princess." Connor leaned down for a quick kiss and then sat snug against Tess on the sofa. "For the celebration." They both stared at her phone, propped up by a pile of novels on the coffee table.

And then the call connected and nearly eight thousand miles away, from far across the ocean, Harry, Isabella and their new baby appeared on the screen.

Tess squealed with delight, so loud Connor said wryly, "Didn't need the hearing in that ear."

Tess jabbed him with an elbow. "Look!" She clapped her hands to her mouth as she stared at the little image of the tiniest, most perfect baby she'd ever seen. The first Harrison grandchild. Her first niece or nephew. The joy swept over her in a wave. This was life, wasn't it? Endings and beginnings, in a continuing and never-ending chain. She'd spent so long living in the past that she hadn't imagined a future as full as this. No matter where, life went on, breaking hearts and then filling them to overflowing.

"Hey, Aunt Tess!" Harry and Isabella waved and the new

mom leaned down to kiss her baby's head. Behind them, a hospital bedhead, some dangling tubes and Isabella's name on a chart hanging above the bed.

"Oh, hello, little sweetie. Oh my God. She or he is absolutely gorgeous." Tess reached for Connor's hand and gripped it like a vice.

"So, what do I have, you two? A niece or a nephew?"

Harry and Isabella exchanged a perfect, loving glance.

"This is Mary Margaret Martenson-Harrison."

"Oh, you guys."

"Mary after Mom," Harry said.

"And Margaret after Maggie, my oldest friend."

"Little Mary Margaret," Tess repeated. "It's perfect. She's perfect. Look at her, Con." Tess laughed, but it came out as a sob and Connor's arm was quickly around her, pulling her close. He kissed her on the top of her head and she wasn't sure that she'd ever felt so happy in her life.

"Congratulations, you two," Connor called out. "She's a little stunner. Lucky for you, mate, she looks like her mum."

Harry chuckled and gazed at his wife. "Iz is a goddamn superstar. The labour went on for hours and when her water broke—"

"Too much information, Harry. How are you feeling, Iz?" Tess asked excitedly. "I suppose you're exhausted and exhilarated all at the same time? You probably just want to stare at her for a couple of years and then fall asleep."

Isabella laughed. "Something like that, Tess. She's six

hours old and already I can't imagine life without her."

Tess looked up at Connor. He returned her gaze and nodded.

"Connor and I have been talking. We thought we might fly over to see you guys. It's been two years since we've been there and we miss you all so much."

Harry and Isabella smiled with delight. "We'd love it," Harry said. "Think you might bring the old man, Amy and Everett with you? This first Harrison grandchild deserves a big celebration, I think. We're planning on having a proper naming ceremony. Think you might want to be a witness, Tess?"

"Oh, Harry." Tears streamed down Tess's cheeks in earnest now. "Of course."

From far away, a tiny set of lungs erupted.

"I think this little one needs something to eat," Isabella said, her eyes wide and slightly panicked.

"We'll leave you to it. We're so proud of you both. I'll be in touch and we'll see you soon."

Tess flopped back on the sofa, still holding Connor's hand. She imagined how Wirra Station would look at the moment. In the height of summer, the watered lawns would be manicured and perfect. The scent of lavender and roses would waft around the grounds, and the weekends would be filled with weddings and declarations of love. If she was back there instead of here in California, she would be on her front porch, watching. California would always be home, but was it possible to hold another place close in your heart, too?

"She's a little cutie, isn't she?" Connor said as he leaned forward to reach for Tess's champagne flute. He passed it to her and then lifted his. "To Mary."

"To Mary," Tess repeated and they clinked glasses. She took a sip and the bubbles exploded in her mouth like fireworks. "Mom would have been so thrilled to share her name with her first grandchild." Tess's eyes drifted to the framed photo on the mantel, one of her mother holding a baby Tess in her arms. Tess was home where she belonged, but on her own terms, living her own dreams.

Connor gazed at her. "You'll always miss her, Tess. And why wouldn't you? Especially at times like these. And little Mary might not have a grandmother, but she's going to have the best aunty in the world, right?"

The flames crackled in the fireplace. The sound of the bubbles popping in the champagne was delicate and sweet. "Hell, yes."

Connor drank up and then squeezed her shoulder. "You'll tell me, won't you, if you change your mind?"

"Change my mind about what?"

"About having kids. I know you said you don't want to have any and I respect that. But if seeing Mary makes you think … or your hormones make you suddenly crazy for a baby … well, all I'm saying is, I'm up for it."

Did he have a direct line to her hormones or something? Did he know her that well? Tess felt the stirring of a rumba deep inside. The truth was, she'd been feeling it ever since Isabella and Harry had announced last year that they were expecting. But Tess was still trying to decipher what that rhythm inside her meant. Was it excitement for them or a deeper longing for a baby of her own?

"I honestly don't know, Connor. But thank you. You've never told me before that you'd like to be a dad. I think you'd be a great one, because I love you and you're awesome and you've had a great role model in your own father but ... anyway."

Tess quickly put her flute down on the coffee table and reached for her laptop. "I'd better email Amy and Everett and Dad's secretary. See if she can get us on flights back to Australia."

Connor slowly pushed the lid closed. "That can wait, princess."

Tess narrowed her eyes at him. "Wait for what?"

Connor reached inside the pocket of his trousers and moved to the floor.

"What are you doing? You're down on one knee," Tess stammered. "And, oh my God, you've got a box."

Connor flipped open the lid and presented it to her. "Tess Harrison. Genius winemaker. Motormouth. Love of my life. Will you marry me?"

The bees were back in her head, swarming, buzzing, making her dizzy. She took the box from his hand and stared at the diamond inside it nestled in black velvet. She didn't know what cut it was, couldn't guess how many carats or anything else about it.

But here's what she knew. When she slipped it on, it fit. It sparkled in the light of the fire. It wasn't a symbol of their love, because she already knew Connor loved her. She knew it in everything he did for her. From a cup of coffee in bed each morning, to the way he still made love to her, to the warm gaze he bestowed on her each day. The same one he was giving her now.

This ring was a promise of a long future together. One she was ready to embrace with open arms and an open heart. And for once, she didn't need to make a speech. Her answer was a simple, "Yes."

"CALM DOWN, TESS." Isabella passed little Mary over to her aunt. "Here, maybe this will help."

"Wait!" Deb rushed up to her side, but was careful to lean away from the baby to protect her mother-of-the-groom outfit. "We don't want her wedding dress to have baby spit on it. Here, let me tuck a little blanket over your shoulder."

Tess looked around the living room of the little cottage she'd called home when she'd been in Wirralong two summers before. Peter and Deb had made it their own since they'd moved in. Turns out, they'd worked picking grapes during the vintage and then decided the attractions of

Wirralong far outweighed the pull of any more adventuring, so they sold their campervan and settled. Peter's carpentry skills made him a handy addition at Wirra Station and Deb occasionally helped Dr. Holly out at the local clinic. Every surface of the cottage was now filled with souvenirs of their travels around Australia, and some from the time they'd spent last year visiting Connor and Tess in California. There was a snow dome with the Hollywood sign in it, a little Golden Gate bridge and a pair of ceramic salt- and pepper-shakers in the shape of oranges. There was also a huge photo of Connor and Tess holding up the label design for the first Motormouth wine, the Mary Margaret Riesling. If anything was going to feel like a home away from home, it was this place. And Tess was so happy to be back here for her wedding.

Deb fussed and clucked over Tess and Tess let her. She loved Connor's mom. "We wouldn't want anything to happen to this gorgeous dress, would we? Here, let me look at you."

Deb held Tess's shoulders and her eyes gleamed as she took in the detail of the simple satin gown. Strapless, it cinched in at her waist and then flowed out in a beautiful skirt. She hadn't wanted any fancy embellishments, that wasn't her. The flat white ballet slippers were perfect and Elsa had done her hair simply, a blow dry into soft curls that brushed her shoulders, with a garland of pink roses on her head. Her makeup was minimal, but mascara highlighted her brown eyes and a deep pink lipstick lifted her smile. All she really needed was her family around her and she had that in spades. Once Tess and Connor had called and told Peter and Deb they were engaged, word spread fast and within half an hour, Isabella had called them in California and offered them a wedding back at Wirra Station.

"Your whole family will be here anyway, Tess, for Mary, so why don't we make it a double celebration? We can organise everything at this end. Deb, Maggie and Elsa have already offered to be the organising committee. Elsa will obviously do your hair and, well, would you like me to officiate at your wedding?"

Tess had been crying so hard at all that news that Connor had taken the phone from her. "We'd love that, Iz." And Tess knew in that moment that she would get through her wedding without her mom, because she would have in her place so many other people who loved her.

"Wait, wait." From across the room, Tess's older sister Amy searched through one of her carry-on pieces of luggage. "It's here somewhere. It had better be. Voila." Her hand emerged from a mess of clothes and shoes holding a velvet box. She opened it, lifted something out and went to Tess, who passed little Mary back to her mother. She whipped off the blanket that had been protecting her dress and gasped.

"They're—"

"Mom's pearls," Amy confirmed. "From her wedding to Dad. I thought you might want to wear them on your wedding day."

"Oh, Amy. They're just perfect."

Amy reached around Tess's neck and fastened the diamante clasp. Tess reached for the smooth pearls and ran her fingers along the strand.

"And no crying, now. You'll smudge your mascara."

Amy, Deb, Isabella and Maggie looked on happily as Tess waved a hand in front of her face to dry her tears. "You are all … the best friends and sister and soon-to-be-mother-in-law a woman could have. I can't believe you've pulled this whole thing together so quickly."

Maggie patted herself on the back. "It's what we do here at Wirra Station. We celebrate love, don't we, Iz?"

Isabella checked her watch. "We do. And you've already kept Connor waiting for five minutes out there. Want to head out and do this?"

"I do." Tess grinned. "See that? I'm getting in some practice before I actually have to say the real I do. I do. I like the sound of it. Now, Iz, you got my instructions to not say 'obey' in the ceremony?"

Isabella rolled her eyes. "I haven't ever included that in my vows. This is the twenty-first century, right?"

"Good. That's good." Tess's pulse raced. She felt a sheen of sweat bead on her brow. This was really about to happen. Oh God. The bees were buzzing in her head again. She felt swoony and not in a good way. "That's not good."

Three pairs of arms rushed to her and pushed her down

on the sofa. Someone lifted her feet on to a stack of pillows and whipped one out from under her head.

"What's happening?" she mumbled.

Deb had taken charge. "You looked a bit woozy there, love. Amy, can you fetch her a glass of cold water? Now, Tess, we're just going to let you lay there a minute or two. Get some blood rushing back to your head, okay? Now, thanks Amy. Here's a cool drink. Finish that whole glass. You're probably a bit dehydrated." Tess did as she was told. Worried faces looked down at her.

Little Mary began to grumble and Isabella clicked her tongue. "I hate to rush you, Tess, but if we don't get started pretty soon, I'll be popping out a boob in the middle of the ceremony."

Tess chuckled, then giggled and then everyone joined in. Laughter echoed around the room and Tess felt better. She sat up. Took a few deep breaths. "I'm fine. Maybe another glass of water? No, on second thoughts. Then I'll have to pee in the middle of the ceremony." She chuckled again as she stood up. She still felt a little lightheaded but maybe that's how every bride felt on their wedding day, as if their feet had lifted off the ground and their head was in the clouds.

"Let's go get me married," she announced.

ISABELLA LED THE women across the green lawns of Wirra

Station to a little clearing by The Woolshed. When Tess saw the arrangement, she wanted to cry all over again. Navy Suit Guy was standing under an arbour decorated with white roses in the lush garden and as she approached, the first notes of music stirred the crowd into standing. He turned and his lips parted in shock at the sight of her and even at this distance she could see his eyes gleaming with unshed tears.

Harry, Connor's first best man, patted him twice on the shoulder. "Hold it together, bro," he said. The second best man, Everett, tried to contain his smile but failed miserably. No doubt he would tease Connor about his tears for the rest of their lives, no matter how old they got.

Amy and Maggie, Tess's bridesmaids, wore their favourite dresses from their own wardrobes because Tess believed in recycling.

It was the perfect day.

Connor reached for her hand and pulled her in close to kiss her cheek. She kissed him back.

The music faded and Isabella stepped up with her clipboard. She cleared her throat and the crowd became silent. Before she could welcome the guests, a pair of kookaburras in a bough of the lemon-scented gum above them began to sing. Everyone turned their eyes to the sky as their trilling, raucous *koo-koo-koo-kah-kah-kah* echoed across the rolling lawns of Wirra Station.

"Welcome, everyone, to the wedding of Tess and Connor."

AFTERWARD, WHEN SHE was in Connor's arms over at The Woolshed, dancing their first dance together, she didn't remember much about the ceremony. It had all been a blur. Except for Isabella's final words.

"Do you, Tess Harrison, take Connor Hawker as your lawfully wedded husband? Do you promise to be true to him, and love him, even when things get imperfect and messy?"

Tess had gasped and Connor chuckled. He'd leaned in. "Hope you like the vows."

"I do," she'd replied with a giggle.

"And do you, Connor Hawker, take Tess Harrison as your lawfully wedded wife? Do you promise to be true to her, and love her, even when things get imperfect and messy?"

"I do," he'd replied.

"By the powers vested in me by the Commonwealth of Australia, I now pronounce you husband and wife."

"Like the song?" Connor twirled her around the dance floor. And that's when she realised. It was a song from the movie *Snow White*. "Some Day My Prince Will Come."

And so it turned out that Tess Harrison did get The Perfect Guy.

The Perfect Guy for her.

The End

If you enjoyed this book, please leave a review at your favorite online retailer! Even if it's just a sentence or two it makes all the difference.

Thanks for reading *Tess* by Victoria Purman!

Discover your next romance at TulePublishing.com.

TULE
PUBLISHING

The Outback Brides of Wirralong

Book 1: *Lacey* by Fiona McArthur

Book 2: *Tess* by Victoria Purman

Book 3: *Jenna* by Barbara Hannay
Coming soon!

Book 4: *Emma* by Kelly Hunter
Coming soon!

Available now at your favorite online retailer!

The Outback Bride Series

Book 1: *Maggie's Run* by Kelly Hunter

Book 2: *Belle's Secret* by Victoria Purman

Book 3: *Elsa's Stand* by Cathryn Hein

Book 4: *Holly's Heart* by Fiona McArthur

Available now at your favorite online retailer!

About the Author

Award-nominated and multi-published Australian contemporary
romance author Victoria Purman loves books, wine, chocolate, sad
country music, hard rock songs and stories with happy ever afters.
Writing romance means she regularly gets to indulge in all those
things – as well as being forced into online pictorial research for
her emotional, funny and smart love stories. In 2014, Victoria was
a finalist in the RuBY Awards (the Romance Writers of Australia's
"Romantic Book of the Year" Awards) for the first book on her
Boys of Summer series for Harlequin MIRA, Nobody But Him.

That same year, she was named a finalist in the category
"Favourite New Author 2013" by the Australian Romance Readers
Association. Most days, she considers herself the luckiest woman
in the world.

Thank you for reading

Tess

If you enjoyed this book, you can find more from all our great authors at TulePublishing.com, or from your favorite online retailer.

TULE
PUBLISHING

Made in the USA
Las Vegas, NV
06 May 2023

71682185R00125